FILTHY VIRGIN

Taboo Trio - Book 1

VIRGINIA ADDISON

Published by Blushing Books
An Imprint of
ABCD Graphics and Design, Inc.
A Virginia Corporation
977 Seminole Trail #233
Charlottesville, VA 22901

Virginia Addison
Filthy Virgin

eBook ISBN: 978-1-64563-831-5
Print ISBN: 978-1-64563-840-7
v1

Chapter 1

Celeste

"Oh shit, baby, that's so *good*. Tell me again," he breathed heavily into the phone. I could hear his groan and the faint sound of him jerking off in the background.

"Harder, Eric, I need it harder!" My voice got higher on the last word and I stifled the giggle that wanted to escape me, when my words elicited another loud groan from the man at the other end. I swallowed my amusement and sketched another line on my drawing.

This particular caricature was coming along nicely, and I grinned to myself while making all the appropriate noises Eric was expecting. I doubted his real name was Eric, but that's what he'd asked me to call him and I did what I was told so I could get paid. Being a phone sex operator was fun at first but had gotten old quickly. I'd taken up drawing a caricature of what I imagined the stranger on the phone would look like and it had made everything much more entertaining. I finished shading the bulging cheeks of the overweight man I'd pictured when he had immediately begun his heavy breathing into the phone that sounded more like asthma than passion.

"Oh…" Eric's grunt of satisfaction rang through the headset I wore, and I made a similar noise like I'd also just orgasmed. He panted for a minute before thanking me and hanging up. I snickered as I clicked the headset off. I rolled my chair over to my laptop and debated on whether I should take another call or just quit for the night. I checked the time, noting it was already 2 a.m. I tapped my fingers on my desk and sighed.

"Just one more call, Celeste, then you can pass out." I spoke out loud to myself and clicked the available icon next to my profile.

I jumped when a call immediately rang through. That happened sometimes, but I was rarely prepared for it. The good news was it always made me sound a little breathless when I answered.

"This is Cassandra, what's your fantasy?" I hated the required opening line, thought it was cheesy and obvious. But whatever paid the bills.

There was silence on the other end, and I frowned but kept my voice light. "Hello? Are you still there?"

A gruff cough sounded in my ear before a low voice spoke. "Sorry, I ah… Didn't expect that opening."

Relaxing, I settled back into my chair. "What did you expect?"

"Nothing so cliché, to be completely honest."

A laugh burst out of me. That's what I'd always thought, but no one had ever said anything about it before. "Next you're going to tell me you've never called a number like this before."

A dark chuckle came through the line and goosebumps popped up on my skin. My mouth dropped open at the reaction. I hadn't responded to the dirtiest of words for months now, ever since my first week of calls had basically desensitized me from getting turned on. Granted, I still held a small feeling of satisfaction that nothing but my voice and words were able to make mysterious men – and a very rare woman – come every time I logged in.

"I haven't, actually." He paused, then continued, "I'm not sure what made me call tonight either. Or why I'm even confessing all this to you."

My lips curved into a smile as I basked in the sound of his voice. I grabbed a pencil and turned to a new page in my sketchbook. "Well, I'm here for whatever you need. If you want to get dirty, or sweet, or just talk, it's up to you. You came here to get what you want, and I'm here to give it to you."

I started to sketch as I waited for him to answer. My pencil glided over the paper, and I could tell this one wouldn't be a humorous caricature. There was something about his voice, his laugh, that wouldn't allow me to draw anything that frivolous. This man was different for some reason.

"What I want, huh? That leaves a lot of options open." He hummed in thought and my nipples perked up at the sound. "Can I ask you some questions?"

I paused, wondering how to answer that. I didn't want to give anything personal away, but his voice compelled me to be honest. I bit my lip and tapped my pencil's eraser on my page.

"Nothing that would make you uncomfortable, Cassandra. You can pass on a question if you feel like it's too close to home."

Relief filled me at his clarification. "Well, in that case, yes. I would be happy to answer some of your questions."

I could hear the satisfied smile in his voice when he responded. "All right, Cassie. Can I call you that?"

"Yes," I replied. Even though Cassandra wasn't my real

name, something about him giving me a nickname warmed me.

"Perfect. Tell me, what makes your pussy wet, Cassie?"

My pencil stuttered on my page, not expecting that question. At. All.

"Uh…" I couldn't get anything out, trying to catch my breath.

His chuckle filled my ear again before he continued, "Little Cassie tongue-tied? I'm just wondering what you like. If you like it when a man pounds into you hard from behind, or if you prefer your thighs around his head while he eats you like dessert."

A small moan escaped me, shocking the hell out of me. I realized then I was wet, my clit throbbing with desire just from a few simple words.

"Are you getting turned on by my questions? Are you a filthy girl who loves getting fucked and talking about it?"

"Oh my god," my voice whispered out. I cleared my throat before finally getting a hold of myself. I wanted to turn him inside out just like he was doing to me, and I knew just how to do it. "As a matter of fact, I do love fucking. I love the feeling of a big, hard cock sliding in and out of my dripping wet pussy while I beg for mercy."

I heard him draw in a sharp breath and I grinned, knowing I'd surprised him with my answer. I don't know why it did; he called a sex line operator after all. He had no idea the things I'd heard or said.

"So you are a filthy girl, my little Cassie? Will you tell me what you look like?"

I hesitated, not wanting to give too much. "Not everything. Pick one thing you want to know."

He barely took a second to think. "What color are your eyes?"

My eyebrows rose. I'd expected him to ask how big my tits were, but he had surprised me again. "They're aqua."

"Aqua? That's specific. Sounds beautiful. If your voice is anything to go by, then you're probably gorgeous all over."

His words made me blush. Fucking blush! I hadn't even blushed last week when a guy asked me to stick a tailed butt plug in his ass and spank him, all while he barked profusely.

"Th-thanks, I guess."

"You're very welcome, Cassandra. Now, that's all I have time for tonight, but you can expect to hear from me again."

"Why?" The question blurted out of me, my body and mind panicked that he would just... leave like this.

"Why? Because you intrigue me, little Cassie. You're funny, obviously intelligent, and your voice makes me hard as fuck. What's not to like?"

My mouth opened and closed, not knowing what the hell to say to that. I only knew I really, really liked the words.

"Until next time, Cassie."

I heard clothes rustling, knowing he was about to hang up when something popped into my head. "Wait!"

My heart pounded, hoping he'd heard my shout. "Yes?"

"Thank God. I just... I was wondering what your name is. What I should call you."

A pause. "Alex."

"Alex. All right." I smiled happily. "Goodnight, Alex."

"Goodnight, filthy Cassandra."

My body heated up at his words and I smiled even bigger as he clicked off. I took off my headset and shut down my profile before turning my computer off. I looked down at my sketchbook, taking in what I'd managed to get down. A strong jaw, teasing lips, and the kind of neck you knew would lead into broad shoulders and a muscled chest.

I hadn't gotten very far before I'd been caught up in his words, and not even a little part of me was sorry for that.

Something about the way he talked, or maybe his voice, pulled at a memory of mine, but it escaped before I could recall it.

"This job just got a thousand times better," I said out loud to no one. I shut off my lights and climbed into bed, wondering when I'd talk to the dark and dirty Alex again.

Chapter 2

Liam

I stared out of my office window without really seeing anything, thinking about the girl I'd talked to on the phone at 2 a.m. because I was so drunk I was past the point of sleeping.

When I'd randomly called a sex line because I'd seen a commercial for it on TV, I had never expected to get someone as fun and dirty as Cassandra, with the sexiest voice I'd heard in a long time—if ever. I hadn't lied when I'd told her the greeting she'd supplied me with was a huge cliché, but it wasn't the reason I'd paused. When she'd answered, her voice had reminded me of someone from my past and it had startled me enough to silence me. But I'd convinced myself there was no way it was her and had gotten my past out of my head. At least, as much as possible while blind drunk.

"Liam!" My best friend's voice jerked me out of my daydreams, and I winced at the resulting ringing of my ears and pounding in my head.

"Fuck, man, do you have to be so loud?"

"Only when you're not listening to a damn thing I'm saying. What's going on with you today?"

"Nothing, I just didn't get much sleep."

Travis and I had been friends for years, and I told him pretty much everything, but I didn't want to talk about Cassandra.

"I'm sure. Just get it together, we need to get this proposal finished and faxed over in the next hour."

"Right. Sorry." I pulled my thoughts away from Cassie and focused on the proposal in front of me, going over the edits Travis and I had talked about for buying out the small company. Thirty minutes later we hung up and I called in my secretary.

"Noelle, please fax this over to Harold Watson. I'm going out to meet my mother for lunch, so—"

"Hold all your calls until tomorrow." A small smile crossed her face and I chuckled.

"You got it, thank you." Noelle snorted and picked up the contract, walking out of the office. Before she got through the doorway, she turned back around.

"Liam…" she began and paused.

I braced myself for her next words. I had a feeling I knew what she was going to say, but I'd let her say it anyway.

"Don't let her get to you. She doesn't deserve anything from you."

I sighed and nodded. "I know. But she's still my mother. She has her issues, but I love her anyway."

She shook her head but didn't say anything else. We'd had this argument before, and it never went anywhere. I knew Noelle was right, my mother didn't deserve the kind of life I provided for her. I shoved the thoughts aside as I grabbed everything I'd need to work from home since I always went straight there after meeting with my mother. It was easier for everyone since I was always in a shitty mood after these rendezvous. Sometimes before, too, hence the drinking last night.

My mother was quite the piece of work. Selfish, materialistic, needy, and the queen of guilt trips. She had her moments of maternal warmth though, so I did what I could to appease her. Our monthly lunch date was one of those things, and it was easy enough to do even if they frustrated the hell out of me. I climbed into my town car and let my mind wander as my driver headed off in the direction of the restaurant.

I wondered if she'd have a new paramour this time around, since every few months she found another one. She'd only had two exceptions– my father who she'd been married to for seven years before he had a sudden heart attack and passed away, and a guy, twelve years ago, whom she'd been married to for six months before they decided on a mutual split. I was just about to turn eighteen when she'd married Henry. I had missed the wedding since it was during my spring break trip with a few friends and it was a quick decision. I didn't even find out they had married until I was back, and my mom was in the process of moving our stuff into Henry's house to live with him and his daughter who'd been just a few years younger than me.

My mind drifted back to the memory of my temporary stepsister, Celeste. Even at sixteen years old, you could tell she was going to grow up and be a knockout. The oddest shade of blueish-green eyes I'd ever seen in a slightly chubby face, a halo of white-blonde curly hair that fell down her back, and her fit form with the promise of curves all served to torture the seventeen-year-old me. The month between the day I moved in and the day I turned eighteen and got out was filled with her pink lips smiling shyly at me, her sweet voice replaying in my mind over and over as I struggled with the attraction to my new stepsister.

I shook my head to get the memories out, wondering why

she was popping into my head again. When Cassandra had answered the phone, it was Celeste who had popped into my mind. They had very similar voices, although Cassandra's was smokier and more mature than Celeste's had been. Granted, it'd also been over a decade since I'd heard Celeste talk, but she had never completely left my mind. A small part of me had always wanted to check in on her, but I didn't want to make her feel awkward because of the situation with our parents.

The car came to a stop and I jerked my eyes open. "Thanks, Tom. I'll be done in about an hour."

"You got it, boss."

I couldn't help but smile just like every time he called me boss. Something about it just felt so 1920's gangster. I let myself out of the car and immediately noticed my mother standing inside the doors. I hated it when she got here before me, even when I was early. It was like she wanted a reason to scold me. I sighed and then plastered a smile on my face, hoping it would distract my mother from lecturing me about my 'tardiness'. She let me kiss her cheek and guide her to our reserved table before saying anything.

"You know how much I dislike being kept waiting." Her cold voice made me stiffen and I met her eyes with my own steady gaze.

"Then you shouldn't have shown up early, Janet," I said, calling her by her first name.

She sniffed but managed to keep her comments to herself. The only time she did that was when she was planning to ask me for something big. I braced myself for the request, but it didn't come. She picked up the menu and glared at it. I knew she was going to order a salad of some sort, since she was always on a diet. She was stick thin and didn't need to lose any more weight, but something had always made her believe she wasn't skinny, or young, or pretty enough. By now I'd given her thousands of dollars that always went to another surgery, another diet plan, another shopping spree. I didn't care what she did with the money as long as she left me alone most of the time.

Our waiter came over and I ordered the marinated sirloin steak, keeping my smirk to myself when Janet ordered a plain salad with no dressing just like I'd expected. I ordered us a bottle of wine I knew she'd like, and the waiter took our menus before heading off to grab it.

"How's business, darling?" Janet's voice was syrupy sweet, and I barely held back my eye roll.

"Really, Mother? 'Darling'?"

She pouted, although with all the Botox she'd had, her face barely moved. "Do you have to turn everything into an argument? I just wanted to check in on you."

I pushed away the twinge of guilt at her words. "You aren't checking on me, you're checking on my money."

"That's ridiculous." She waved away my words and before I could respond the waiter returned. I tried to tamp down the frustration that was amplified by my lack of sleep. I nodded at the waiter to let him know he could pour the wine and I resigned myself to the next longest hour of my life.

Janet prattled on about her so-called friends and what sort of trouble they had gotten themselves into recently, and I nodded along while mostly ignoring her words. A husky, feminine voice was apparently the only one my brain was hearing today.

"Liam? Did you hear what I said?"

"Sorry, Mother, I must have missed that last part. What was it?"

She sniffed in indignation and I gritted my teeth in frustration. Usually when she did that, it meant she was expecting me to coax out whatever information she wanted to tell me anyway. I opened my mouth but was surprised when she interrupted me.

"I *said*, I need you to do me a favor."

I raised an eyebrow, not surprised. "How much do you need?"

"I don't mean money."

"What?" Her words shocked the hell out of me. "It's always about money though."

"Not always! What kind of thing is that to say to your mother?" she protested, but her cheeks pinkened and I knew the words were all for show.

"Well, if it's not about money, what else could it possibly be?" I lifted my drink to take a sip.

"Celeste."

Every muscle in my large frame seized, and I set my drink back down without drinking any of it. "Come again?"

"Are you hard of hearing, Liam? It's Celeste. I need you to hire her."

"Hire Celeste? The daughter of the man you were married to, twelve years ago, for six months?"

"Yes."

I paused, picking up my drink once again and taking a few huge gulps. "Why?"

My mother looked away from me, staring out the window with a blank look on her face. "Henry passed away a few months ago, and I bet she's struggling under the pressure of trying to cover his medical bills and finish her degree." She looked back at me now. "You're successful, and I could've sworn you mentioned something about Travis needing a new assistant the last time we had lunch."

My mouth was hanging open slightly, trying to register her words. My mother, who I begrudgingly loved but knew was not much more than a pretty face and vicious words, was asking me to help someone else.

"First of all, how do you even know about all that? Isn't Henry about four husbands ago?"

If Janet hadn't had as much work done as she did, her face would've easily turned into a scowl of disapproval. "I may not be the best mother, Liam Alexander Whiscombe, but I am still your mother. No need to be rude." I bent my head towards her in silent apology, which she accepted. "Henry and I did not work out as a married couple, but he was kind. After splitting we ended up keeping in touch."

There was a wistfulness to my mother's voice I had never heard before. From what I could remember of Henry, he had seemed like a nice enough guy. Not poor, not rich, but he was always laughing and carrying on about his daughter. Celeste. Who seemed to be a running theme today.

"Well, what do you think?" Janet interrupted my thoughts, and I focused back on her.

"Is she qualified? Do you think she could handle the workload?"

"I'd say so. Henry said she always did well in school, at the top of her class every time. Whatever she doesn't know I'm sure she can learn quickly."

"Why are you so interested in her? No offense meant, Mother, but this help-the-needy thing you've got going on isn't your usual style."

"What, I can't change?"

I scoffed, thankful our food had begun to arrive so I wouldn't have to answer that question. Truthfully, I didn't think she could change. Not for anyone.

I thanked the waiter as he laid our plates on the table and silently floated off to leave my mother and me alone again. She took a couple small bites before getting right back to her request.

"Liam, please. I..." she trailed off and I looked up at her, taking in her demeanor. She was avoiding my gaze, staring down at her food instead of looking me in the eyes with her usual fake pleasantness. "I know I'm not the warmest person, and I know I've done you wrong. And even though my marriage with Henry didn't last, I really did care for him. I'd like to repay his kindness somehow by helping his daughter. Will you help?"

I was fucking shocked. I had never heard my mother talk like that about anyone or anything, and even though it was extremely hard for me to believe it was the truth, something in her voice convinced me.

"All right, Mother. I'll have Travis call her for an interview if you give me her info. I can't promise more than that though, if she can't take it then that's not my fault."

She was smiling brightly at me. "Thank you, Liam! I'll give you her info before you leave. Now, one smaller favor. There's this bag I saw the other day and I just know it would go perfectly with my new dinner dress, and…"

I chuckled reluctantly as I tuned her out. Happy to see Janet hadn't been taken over by aliens after all. Some things never changed.

Chapter 3

Celeste

"Another extra-large margarita for the miss," a voice said beside me. I opened my eyes to see a giant bird holding out a margarita to me by its claw, and I gratefully took it.

"Thanks, Barry," I said pleasantly. He opened his beak and a shrill sound left it, startling me. I looked back over at him. "What was that?"

He looked at me, his beak opening with the same shrill sound, making me fall out of my chair into the sand.

I hit the ground with a jerk and my eyes flew open, waking me up from the weirdest dream I'd ever had. A giant talking bird named Barry, serving me margaritas? I wasn't even sure I wanted to know what that meant. The shrill sound from my dream went off again near my ear, and I realized it was my phone ringing.

I hurried to pick it up, not recognizing the number displayed on the screen, but taking the chance with it anyway.

"Hello?"

"Is this Ms. Celeste Thompson?" a man's voice said through the phone, sure and strong.

"Uh, yes?"

A small pause. "Well, is that an answer or are you not sure?"

I wanted to smack myself in the head at the humor in his voice. "Yes, this is Celeste Thompson. Can I help you?"

"That's kind of what I was hoping. I'd like to offer you a job." Suspicion filled me and I let his question hang in the silence, waiting for him to continue. "Ah, a real job. Nothing weird."

I snorted into the phone. "Honestly, this whole thing is a little weird already."

"Yeah, sorry. I'm not the best at this. My name is Travis Coffman, and I work at the Whisman Offices. I'm looking for a new assistant, and your information was given to me by a mutual… friend."

"Whisman Offices?" I asked the question aloud, wondering why it sounded so familiar. "What kind of company is it?"

"We're an art gallery and auction business. We cater to well-known artists from all over the U.S., as well as local artists just getting started."

"Hmm. And what would my job requirements be?"

"Inventory, event scheduling, keeping my work and personal life schedules in sync, other paperwork-type duties."

I tapped my finger on my leg, contemplating the offer. Hundreds of thoughts swirled through my mind, along with a nagging sense of missing a piece of the puzzle.

My silence must have worried Travis, since he spoke up before I could say anything. "I'd like to offer the position starting at twenty-three dollars an hour. It would be a Monday through Friday job, with some weekend and night events. Any events outside of normal work hours would be time and a half."

My jaw dropped in amazement. A steady full-time job, that paid well with seemingly good benefits, which would help me lessen my hours at the phone sex job without taking a hit financially? I'd probably have to still do some time on the phone since I had so many bills and debt to get rid of, but with this job I'd be able to start enjoying my life.

"Would it be unprofessional of me to accept the job right away?" I asked the question half-seriously and was relieved to hear him chuckle.

"Not at all. My current assistant will be leaving at the end of this week, so if you'd like to get started tomorrow, I can have her train you on the more complicated items before she takes off for new adventures."

"Then I would like to accept."

"Perfect! Give me your email address, and I will send some paperwork, and more information about the company and position, so you're well prepared for tomorrow."

"Thank you, Mr. Coffman. I really appreciate the offer." The relief was evident in my voice, and I could hear the warm smile in his next words.

"Travis, please. And you're helping me just as much, Ms. Thompson."

"Call me Celeste."

"You got it. See you bright and early tomorrow."

We hung up, and I sat in my bed in shock. I pinched my thigh just to make sure I wasn't still dreaming, and it hurt enough to tell me it was completely real.

I squealed in excitement, jumping off my bed and dancing around my room. I immediately dialed my best friend Madison to tell her the great news. It rang a couple of times, and when she said hello I couldn't help but just let out a shriek of excitement.

"Ahh! Celeste, why are you screaming into my ear? Is everything okay? You're not dying, are you?"

I laughed hard, trying to find the breath to answer her. "No, I'm not dying! I just got a job! A real one!"

Her shriek of excitement matched my own, and I was sure our decibels were hurting dogs' ears everywhere. "That is amazing, Celeste! How'd you manage to find one in between all your side stuff?"

I paused. "You know, I'm not really sure. I got the call just now, and the man I talked to, Travis, said a mutual friend of ours recommended me."

"Really? Who?"

"I don't know, I completely forgot to ask."

"Well, what's the company name? Maybe I can help."

"They're called Whisman… Offices or something. It's an art gallery and auction house I guess."

"Doesn't sound familiar. Let me Google it."

"Ooh, good idea. I'll check too."

We chatted casually while we both pulled up our computers to check the company out. I pulled up the site, and my eyes widened at the beautiful pieces of art on their home page. I scrolled slowly, taking it all in. Madison's voice brought me out of my head a minute later.

"Well, I don't think there's any connection to us. Maybe an old friend of your dad's or something?"

I scanned through a couple more pictures, responding to Madison absently, "I doubt it. My dad wasn't really an arts and crafts type of person."

"True. It says here the company is co-owned by a Travis Coffman and a Liam Whiscombe, and they started it about seven years ago."

My blood froze at her words. *No way. It couldn't be.*

Madison was still talking about the company when I interrupted her, "Did… Did you say Liam? Liam Whiscombe?"

"Uh, yeah. Why does that name sound familiar?"

"Where are you seeing this?"

"On the last page, under 'Company Information'. Wait–" she paused and I could practically hear something click in her mind. "Didn't you have a stepbrother once named Liam?"

I clicked on the last page and my breath caught in my chest when I tried to breathe. "Yes. Liam Whiscombe."

I was looking at my stepbrother's face for the first time in years. Well, ex-stepbrother. His mom and my dad had been married for only six months when I was about sixteen, but I'd never forgotten about him. He'd been the most beautiful man I'd ever seen, and I was obsessed from the moment he first stepped into my house. I hadn't told a soul about my infatuation, and I was so very glad about that at this moment.

"No way. Your stepbrother owns this company? That's crazy."

"Well, he's not my stepbrother anymore, but yeah, apparently he does. But how... I mean, we barely even saw each other when our parents were married, so I highly doubt he'd be recommending me for this job."

"Right, but how else would Travis had gotten your information?"

"I honestly have no idea–" I paused and we both were silently thinking. "Mads... do you think I should call back and turn the job down?"

"What? No! I mean, maybe it'll be awkward at first, but you need this job. You need the freedom it'll provide so you can start living like you're in your twenties."

"I guess you have a point." *Even though you have no idea part of my hesitation is because of my old crush.*

"Trust me, Celeste. Take the job. Everything will be fine."

"Okay, okay. You convinced me."

"Good, now stop worrying and enjoy the fact you have a regular job!"

I couldn't help the laugh that escaped before hanging up with her, my relief and happiness surging through me once again. She was right; this is exactly what I'd been hoping for all along. It was even in my field of interest, which was a huge blessing. Now I'd be able to quit my odd jobs, and even the phone sex one sooner rather than later.

I paused at that thought, Alex's voice and promise to call me again coming to mind. *Maybe I would keep that job just a little longer*, I thought to myself with a satisfied smile.

Chapter 4

Celeste

Despite the reassurances from Madison the night before, now that I was walking into the building of my new job, I wish I'd called and turned them down after all. I tried to keep my poker face on, pleasant smile in place, but I was shaking in my worn-out heels. I'd pulled out the only office sensible outfit I had this morning, knowing I was going to have to go buy more ASAP. All I had was a pair of slightly scuffed black three-inch heels, a black pencil skirt I'd had since high school which was now a little tight, and one white button up shirt.

I walked up to the front desk where a beautiful woman around the same age as myself sat. She looked up as I opened the door, a polite smile on her face. I tried to hide my nervousness as I smiled back and introduced myself.

"Hi, I'm Celeste. I guess I'm supposed to start today with Travis."

"Ah yes, I heard about that! I'm Noelle," she said while

standing up to take my outstretched hand. "I'm not usually at this desk, but the front reception guy is out sick today."

I let the surprise show on my face as she came around the desk, motioning for me to follow her. "What do you usually do here then? Sorry if that's rude," I hurriedly added.

She let out an easy laugh. "Not at all. I'm the other owner's assistant."

I was glad she wasn't looking at me as I felt my face begin to color. Casually as possible I commented, "Oh, you mean Liam?"

"Yes. Those two can be a handful, but they're great to work for."

"That's relieving to hear," I said with obvious relief. She turned to look at me and grinned.

"It doesn't hurt they're both hot as hell," she whispered, before knocking on the door we'd stopped in front of.

"Enter." The serious, somber voice brought back all the nerves, but Noelle snorted next to me before turning the knob and pushing the door open.

"Why are you so weird, Travis?" Some of the nerves dissipated with her words as I followed Noelle into the room, taking a deep breath before stepping out from behind her.

A hearty laugh filled the room, and I froze as I took in the sight before me. Travis was sitting at his desk in his office, a giant smile on his face as he and Noelle teased each other. He was obviously attractive; well-built, tall, blond hair and blue eyes that sparkled with humor.

But it was the man who had stood up as we walked in, turning around slowly, who held my attention completely. Noelle and Travis' voices fading into the background as I stared into a pair of dark eyes I hadn't seen in twelve years.

Liam had grown up well. My lady bits whimpered at the look in his eyes as his gaze swept over me. *Too fucking well.*

He'd been attractive at eighteen years old, but now that

he was in his thirties, he'd turned into what Madison and I called a visual vitamin. As in, you needed a daily dose to keep your health. He was a bit taller, had bulked out a bit more, and had grown out his jet-black hair from a buzz cut to something more stylish that had the front of his hair flopping onto his forehead in a way that made my fingers itch to push it back.

My already tight skirt felt tighter than usual as we continued to stare at each other, and I could feel the blush heating up to danger levels of red on my cheeks. Thankfully, Travis stood up and pulled my attention, breath rushing into my lungs as I broke eye contact.

"Celeste, I'm so glad you accepted the position. It's going to be a lot to take in in the next three days, but if what my buddy over here told me about you is true then you should be just fine."

I cut my eyes to Liam in question for a moment, before focusing on Travis again. "And what exactly has he told you?"

"You're hard-working. Reliable. A quick learner and adaptable. Did well in school." Travis was very matter of fact about it, like he trusted Liam's word without hesitation.

My only question was how the hell would Liam know any of that about me since we hadn't seen each other or spoken in over a decade. I kept that thought to myself though, not wanting to ruin this chance before I even got started.

Faking a confidence I didn't feel, I replied, "Well, that's all true. He forgot to mention I'm a three-time Nobel Peace Prize recipient, however."

I bit back the laughter that wanted to burst out of me when the eyes of all three bugged out of their heads at that. Moments later, Liam started to chuckle and my senses perked up at the sound. A zing went through me when he threw his head back and laughed loudly, catching onto my bullshit.

"Oh man, Celeste," he said after letting it out. "I forgot

you had a way of spitting out something ridiculous like that with a completely straight face."

I grinned back, finally letting out my own laugh. My body warmed to think he'd not only noticed that about me while our parents had been married, but even remembered it.

I turned back to Travis, still chuckling. "Sorry, I tend to tell ridiculous stories like that when I'm nervous and need to break the tension."

He'd been laughing along with Liam and Noelle when they realized I was messing with them, and I began to relax. If they could handle that side of me, then I was pretty sure I would fit in well here.

"No worries. I appreciate a good sense of humor and honesty like that." He glanced at the watch on his wrist before continuing, "Emma should be here in a few minutes, and I can have her start going over everything with you. Would you like a coffee or something before she gets here?"

"A water would be great actually, if you have some."

"I can show her around a little." I turned to face Liam, surprised at the offer.

"Sure, that'd be fine. I've got to take a phone call in a minute, and since Noelle is manning the front today that leaves you or Emma to do it. And since you don't do shit around here..."

Liam rolled his eyes before stepping closer to me. "Ignore him. He has no idea what he's talking about."

I couldn't help but giggle at their easy banter even though the thought of walking around with Liam, alone, filled me with nerves. The feelings I'd done my best to hide twelve years ago were starting to resurface, and I couldn't let that happen and end up ruining the best chance of a job I'd had in years.

Liam came to my side and placed a hand on the small of my back, guiding me out of the room behind Noelle.

Although his hand rested in a spot completely appropriate,

the heat of his hand through my shirt and undershirt made my skin tingle with awareness. The tingles increased when his hand pressed harder into my back, encouraging me to turn down a hallway to my left. After I turned, he dropped his hand and I was filled with equal parts relief and disappointment.

We walked down the hall in silence, and it was starting to wear on my nerves. I wasn't great at handling silence well in the first place, and now, here I was walking down the hall with my ex-stepbrother whom I was undeniably still attracted to after twelve years. I wanted to break the silence, but I didn't even know where to begin.

"This is the break room area," he said in a soft voice, reaching over me to push open a door.

I barely even looked at the room. My eyes followed him to the fridge, where he pulled out a bottle of water and popped the top, handing it to me. I twisted the lid the rest of the way off and took a few large gulps, trying to quench the dryness of my throat. I could feel him watching me, and when my head tilted back down I saw him staring at me.

I let out a nervous laugh as I twisted the lid back on. "So... this is weird, right?"

The corner of his mouth twitched, but he didn't full on smile. "Yeah, it is," he paused, and I watched as his face softened. "I'm really sorry about your dad, by the way."

I nodded in thanks, my throat too choked up to really answer. It was still hard getting used to the fact he was gone. He'd been battling cancer for a while, and though we thought he would beat it, he ended up dying about a year ago.

"How's your mom doing?" My voice only cracked once, and I cleared my throat.

He snorted. "Nothing's changed with her, I'm afraid."

I let out a smile. "Yeah, I'm not surprised. I know she and my dad kept in touch after splitting, since he would talk about

25

her sometimes. He always found her antics amusing." And now that I thought about it, maybe that was how Travis had heard about me. Made sense.

"Well someone's got to, I suppose." A wry smile crossed his face, and then he seemed to shake off the topic. "Anyway, let me give you a tour of the rest of the place, and then I'll bring you back to Emma for some training."

"You got it, boss." I smiled at him cheekily and he merely grunted in response, holding the door open for me as I walked out.

I stepped out into the hallway and then turned, waiting for him to show me where to go next. His eyes flickered up to my face, and I could have sworn he was checking out my ass. I shrugged it off though, since I figured there was no way that was possible.

Walking around with Liam was surreal. I could hardly concentrate on everything he was telling me, my thoughts a whirlwind inside my head. Thankfully, I'd always been interested in art so when he brought me to the gallery and showrooms, I was able to forget about him momentarily while I took everything in.

By the time he brought me back to Emma's desk I'd started to get used to being around him again. It was going to be a little odd for a bit, but if I could keep my attraction to him in the back of my mind, I could figure this out and really enjoy this job.

Hopefully.

Chapter 5

Liam

After dropping Celeste off with Emma, I walked back to my office for a little time to cool down. I nodded at Noelle on my way past her desk, not wanting to start up a conversation in this state.

I shut my door behind me once I made it inside and leaned against it, taking a few deep breaths.

"Fuck," I muttered out loud while adjusting my cock in my pants. Seeing Celeste all grown up shouldn't have surprised me, but holy hell... I couldn't help but remember the way her gorgeous eyes widened slightly when we stood face to face for the first time in twelve years, and how that black skirt hugged her curves perfectly, the white shirt slightly straining at the buttons around her tits.

I groaned, pushing away from my door to take a seat at my desk, hoping to use work to get this erection to go away. I'd managed to keep her slightly in front of me during the tour, so hopefully she hadn't noticed the bulge in my pants while walking around. The downside to that was the fact her swaying hips had mesmerized me, her tight ass only serving to keep me hard the whole time.

Goddamnit, I should not be this attracted to my stepsister. *Ex-stepsister*, my brain decided to remind me. I gritted my teeth while I argued with myself.

That doesn't make a difference, I replied. *She's still off limits.*

I pulled up the spreadsheet I'd been working on the day before, using the numbers and data to take my mind off the woman I'd ignored my sudden and unsuitable attraction to years ago. I was able to do it then; it shouldn't be a problem for me now. I was more mature and had more control over my body and my mind by this point. Right?

Wrong.

I was so very wrong. The last three days had been some kind of weird torture I was sure monkey demons from Hell had devised for me, just for their own entertainment. It was Saturday, and thankfully we didn't have anything going on today at the office, so we were closed. But the last three days Celeste had been unintentionally provoking thoughts I had no business thinking.

She must have been trying to tempt me, because on her second day she came in wearing a red sheath dress that hugged every single fucking curve I wanted to feel in my hands. I'm sure it would've looked perfectly fine on anyone else; it was an appropriate length ending at just above her knees, with cap sleeves and a neckline that didn't show any cleavage.

But on Celeste it merely covered her curves like gift wrapping, tempting me to rip that dress off and see exactly what she was hiding under it. I'm sure by this point she thought I was ignoring her, but I didn't want to make the workplace feel awkward for her, at a new job I knew she needed, by staring at her constantly. I was surprised she hadn't asked me how her information had gotten to us. Either she didn't care, or she already knew.

My stomach growling brought me out of the memories of the last few days, and on a whim I decided to go out to a nearby bar to get some food, maybe find someone to take my mind off a woman I shouldn't want.

I stepped into the bar, unsurprised at the amount of people inside since it was a Saturday night. Walking to the bar, I didn't see the person moving to the edge of the dance floor until she spun into my side.

"Oh my God, I'm sorry! I didn't see– You!"

I'd pulled the woman into my arms in order to stop her from falling onto the floor after bumping into me, and a small part of me was starting to regret it now that I'd figured out whom it was.

Celeste's bright eyes were wide in shock, staring up at me. My arms reflexively tightened around her, pulling her tighter into my body. A sharp intake of quiet breath passed between us, and the urge to bend down and take her mouth filled me suddenly. I started to move, and then another voice startled the both of us, Celeste jumping back out of my grasp leaving me with a sense of loss.

"Celeste! That was a close one!" A peppy, slender but shapely woman with dark red hair and light green eyes linked her arm with Celeste's, gazing up at me with slightly unfocused eyes and I realized she was completely drunk. I glanced over at Celeste again to check on her, and bit back a groan at the way her cheeks had pinkened, her gaze avoiding mine.

"Well, aren't you a tall drink of water." The other woman's loudly muttered words drew my eyes back over to her, an amused smirk twitching at my lips. Her eyes grew large and she slapped a hand over her mouth when she realized she'd spoken out loud.

"You think so? I've always felt I was more of a whiskey guy than water," I replied with a chuckle.

Celeste rolled her eyes when her friend started to giggle. "Sorry about her, she's had a bit too much to drink tonight."

"No worries, sis."

Celeste's cheeks turned even pinker at the casual mention of the fact we'd been related at one point.

"Sis? Oh! That's why you look familiar!" A finger poked me in the chest, and I held back a wince at the sharp dig. "This is your new boss-slash-stepbrother, right?"

"Well, he's not technically my boss, Madison. Or my step-brother," she added with a glare in my direction.

Madison waved away her words as she wobbled on her heels. "Technically, shmeck... shpeckally... ah hell, you know what I'm trying to say." She grabbed my arm, with a grip which surprised me, and started dragging Celeste and me across the dance floor, pushing people out of the way while continuing to yell over her shoulder, "Come meet our other friends! Well, one is my husband, but that's beside the point." She kept jabbering on, but I couldn't hear her anymore over the music and the crowd.

I was amused with the whole thing right up until we stopped at a table with two other men, one standing and catching Madison as she flung herself into his body, the other watching me with wary eyes as Celeste sat in the chair next to him. I took him in with a sharp gaze, jealousy razing through me as he slung an arm casually around Celeste. She turned her head towards him and I tried to gauge their relationship, but I couldn't read the look on her face.

Madison unwound her body from whom I was assuming was her husband before making the introductions. Pointing to the man gazing at her and proving me right, she said, "This is

Luke, my husband. That's his brother, Anthony. We all grew up together, so we've been friends for a long time. Guys, this is Celeste's new boss, but not really, who is also her stepbrother."

"Ex," Celeste and I chimed in at the same time. Our eyes met once again and a heat, I swore I imagined, passed between us before she glanced away.

"Ex-stepbrother," Celeste repeated. "His name is Liam."

Luke reached across the table to shake my hand as I took the now empty chair between Celeste and Madison. "It's good to meet you, man," he said casually.

I nodded in acknowledgement and then reluctantly turned to the brother and extended my hand to him as well. He pulled his arm from around Celeste, and I couldn't help but squeeze his hand, a tad harder than normal, in mine.

As fucked up as it might be for me to want Celeste as much as I did, it didn't stop me from getting annoyed that another man was touching her, even casually. When we let go of the tense handshake, I was able to relax slightly when Anthony didn't sling his arm around the object of my obsession again.

"So, what's the story with the whole step-siblings thing?" Luke voiced the question I was sure most of them had been wondering.

"There's not much to tell, honestly. Twelve years ago, her dad was married to my mom. After six months they got divorced, and we haven't seen each other since then. I remember seeing you guys around once, but we never actually met each other."

Celeste chimed in at this point. "We never really saw each other." She turned towards me. "You were gone a lot, and then suddenly one day you were moved out."

I kept my face blank as I nodded, but my blood heated with her words. I remembered with perfect clarity the day I moved out. I'd done it when I knew no one was going to be home, because I didn't want to deal with my mom trying to convince me otherwise, and her dad telling me I didn't have to go.

Mostly though, I didn't want to know if Celeste would look at me with her large eyes begging me to stay. But I'd known I couldn't stay there any longer. Not after what had happened the week before.

Home from a long day at work, I was relieved to see my mom and Celeste's dad were out. It was a Friday night, and Celeste was usually hanging out with her friends. It looked like all the lights were out, so I was guessing I'd have the place to myself. I went inside to my room and stripped, grabbing a towel and heading to the bathroom Celeste and I were sharing temporarily since hers was being remodeled. Flipping on the light, the first thing my gaze went to was the pair of silky white panties she must have missed the last time she showered.

I averted my gaze, something inside me twitching at the sight of the innocent panties. She was my sixteen-year-old stepsister for God's sake, I shouldn't be attracted to her. She was quiet, but quick-witted. I'd heard her dry sense of humor and it always made me chuckle. Every time I laughed, her cheeks would redden, and she would hide her face in her white-blonde hair, a pleased smile on her lips.

I showered quickly, wanting to get into bed before everyone showed back up and get some sleep. I stepped out of the bathroom fifteen minutes later, falling into bed. I didn't know how long I was sleeping when a sound woke me up. I rubbed my eyes, then checked the time. It was around midnight, so I figured I'd just heard Celeste coming home.

I don't know why I got out of bed. Something pulled me to my door, making me open it and look down the hallway to Celeste's room. I was surprised to see Celeste's door cracked open, the light off. Figuring it was nothing, I dismissed it. I was closing my door again when a sound caught my attention, and I paused in the doorway. Another sound came from her room, and curiosity got the better of me. I walked towards her door and was about to quietly call her name when mine suddenly filled the silence.

I froze, fingertips on her door.

"Liam…" My name hit my ears again, the breathy moan making my body automatically react. I pressed lightly on the door, needing to confirm with my eyes what I thought I was hearing. It opened enough for me to see Celeste on her bed, covers shoved to the side, wearing nothing but moonlight, a thin tank top and another pair of those silky white panties I'd seen in the bathroom. Her legs were parted, one hand inside her underwear and the other teasing her hard nipple under her shirt. I froze, heart stuttering at the sight. Blood pumped south as her quiet voice filled the air, body arching in her bed as she got closer to coming.

Seconds later neurons fired in my brain, snapping me back to reality. I jerked away from her open door, quickly hurrying back to my own room as quietly as possible. I let out a growl of frustration as soon as my door was shut, willing myself to forget what I'd just seen. It was a natural reaction, to get turned on when you heard the sounds I had and seen what I'd seen, but I was still disgusted with myself.

I now knew Celeste touched herself to thoughts of me. I knew my body responded to it, but I still had morals. I knew at that second, for both mine and Celeste's sake, I had to get out of there. I had to protect her from herself, and from me. If that meant leaving, then that's what I would do.

I tuned back into the conversation as the memory of that day faded, seeing Celeste was watching me, her bottom lip caught between her teeth as she studied me. So much had changed in the last twelve years, but my desire to protect her was one thing that hadn't changed. I still wanted to make sure she was kept safe. But now, I wasn't sure if that was stronger than the need that had popped up between us now. And if she felt anything like she did back then, I was guessing I had quite the challenge on my hands.

Chapter 6

Celeste

I fiddled with my headset, spinning my pencil between my fingers at my desk at home and stared at my computer screen. I'd been sitting here for a few hours, just waiting. Really, I'd been waiting for a few days. It was almost 2 a.m., and I was starting to feel like an idiot.

I'd thought I would hear from Alex by now, but maybe he was just being kind about calling back for me last time we talked. That, or he was playing hard to get. I scoffed out loud and dropped my pencil onto my sketchpad, leaning back in my chair and rubbing my face in frustration.

Between the nerves of working with Liam and staying up late every night to see if Alex would call, I was a mess. A bundle of nerves, almost constantly wet at the anticipation of talking to Alex battling with the memory of the way Liam looked in his work suits.

My eyes began to get heavy, and I sighed with resignation that it would be another night of disappointment. I took the headset off and set it down, reaching for the mouse to say I was offline and unavailable for calls. Just as I was about to click off, a notification popped up on the screen and made me jump.

"Customer Alex *requesting private chat. Would you like to accept?"*

My heart rate went from zero to one hundred in point three seconds, and I moved my mouse away from the logout button and over to 'yes' so fast I almost sprained my wrist.

The messenger app popped up, a message from Alex there already.

"Hey Cassie. Sorry it took me a few days; I've been a bit preoccupied. Hope you didn't forget about me?"

There was no fighting the giant smile on my face, relief flooding me as I typed back.

"Sorry, who is this?" I giggled to myself and watched as three dots indicating he was typing popped up.

"I'm the one who made your pussy wet when we talked on the phone last, Cassie."

My cheeks flushed, and I debated what to respond with. Before I could reply, he started typing again.

"Don't try to deny it. I could tell that little moan you let out was a real one, not faked like I'm sure it is for all the other men you end up on the phone with."

Another one of those little moans slipped from my mouth reading those words. God, this man was dangerous.

"Maybe I'm so good at my job you wouldn't be able to tell either way."

"If you give me access to your private line I can assure you you wouldn't have to fake a single thing with me, whether I could tell or not."

I tapped my fingers on the desk, contemplating. Honestly, I didn't see how it could go wrong for me. He'd be paying extra for the private line tonight and any other night he called. The only thing was he'd be able to reach me through my phone app, which meant he could contact me at any time. I had never given anyone access to it, but he tempted me like no other. Before I could decide either way, he started to type another message.

"Please, Cassandra. I miss your voice. I want to have access to it without having to go through all these channels. I want to hear it late at night when I can't sleep, in the mornings when you haven't fully woken up, and maybe even in the middle of the day where all you can say is 'yes' or 'no' because you don't want anyone else to know what you're doing."

Fuck. My nipples had hardened, my panties getting wetter with every word I read. By the time I got to the end of the message, I was convinced. It might be a fucking terrible decision, but I gave him the number for my private line, without another word. Seconds later, it rang through on my phone and I accepted the call.

"Thank fuck, Cassie, I wasn't sure you were going to say yes."

A throaty laugh left me. "I wasn't sure either for a minute."

"What made you give in?" His voice was dark, raspy, and I closed my eyes to better enjoy it.

"I'm... I don't know."

"I think you do, dirty Cassandra." He paused, but I had no idea what to say. Imagine that— the phone sex operator, at a loss for words. "I think you want to talk to me just as much as I want to talk to you."

"I suppose that's a possibility."

"Hmm. Where are you?"

"I'm in my room."

"Details, Cassie. Where in your room? What were you doing before I called?"

"I'm at my desk. I was drawing." Sort of. I hadn't gotten much done since I'd mostly been focused on waiting to hear from him. Not that he needed to know that.

"Really?" Interest and a little surprise colored his voice. "What do you like to draw?"

"Anything. Everything. Whatever comes to mind."

"I'd like to see something someday. But for now, I have another question for you."

I'd become a little flustered when he said he wanted to see my drawings, so grateful he'd moved on quickly. I didn't even care what the question was; I'd never shown anyone my drawings or other art, not even Madison. If he seriously asked to see them in that voice of his, how was I supposed to turn him down, despite my reluctance to share that side of myself?

"And what question is that?"

"What are you wearing?" I could hear the smile in his voice, and I laughed lightly at the typical question.

"Really? That's the question you're going to go with?"

"Yep. But here's the catch; I want to know what you're really wearing, not what you think I want to hear."

"If you insist." I looked down at myself before beginning. "I'm wearing light gray sweatpants that are a few sizes too big because I like the comfort. A Peanuts t-shirt on top."

"Cute."

"I guess. What I really like about the shirt though," I continued, as I lowered my voice to a more seductive tone, "is I've worn it so much the neck is stretched out enough that it kind of just hangs off one of my bare shoulders, and it's basically see-through. And since I'm not wearing a bra underneath..."

I heard his sharp intake of breath as I trailed off, and let the self-satisfaction fill me.

"I can just imagine the way it'd tempt my eyes to follow the line of your collar bone to where the shirt molds to the curves of your full, delicious tits."

"You'd definitely be able to see the dark shadows of my nipples, and the way they stand out through the thin cotton, begging for your hands or your tongue."

"*Shit*, Cassie." His groan filled my ear before he spoke

again. "I need you to go to your bed. Take your sweats off and lay down on your back."

My body was moving before he even finished the demand. Letting my pants fall to my feet, I stepped out of them and fell back into my pillows.

"I'm there, Alex."

"Good girl." I let out a whimper at the two words, never knowing they would have that kind of effect on me. "I want you to do everything I tell you unless it makes you completely uncomfortable. If it does, just let me know and I'll switch gears."

"Okay," I agreed with more enthusiasm than I really wanted to show. His quiet laugh confirmed he knew exactly how excited I was for whatever was about to happen. I lay on my bed, wetter than I'd ever been before, waiting for the instructions I was sure were going to make me come... *hard.*

Chapter 7

Liam

God, this woman... I was already hard as fuck, imagining her lying in her bed in nothing but a see-through shirt and panties. Obviously, I had no idea what she looked like except for the color of her eyes, but my brain helpfully supplied a vision of a curvy woman with long blonde hair. I ignored the resemblance of the imaginary woman to Celeste, choosing instead to focus on making Cassandra come.

"Do you have both hands free?"

"I do." Her voice held a slight tremble, and I bit back a groan at the sound.

"Good. I want you to run your fingers over your skin, starting at your thighs. Lightly trace invisible patterns, working slowly up until you reach the edge of your panties. While you do that, tell me how it feels."

"I feel more sensitive than I thought I would, the feeling of my fingertips teasing my skin and lighting up my senses. My skin is soft, warm..."

I let out a sound of approval. "Now skim them up your stomach, pressing your shirt up along the way. Imagine it's my hands touching you, learning how you respond, watching your face."

The sound she made was indescribable, but it made my need ratchet up higher. I couldn't resist pulling my cock out of my boxer briefs, the only thing I was wearing at the moment, and wrapping my hand around it tight at the base.

"Now I want you to take your shirt off, relax into your pillows, and run your fingers across your neck, trace your collarbones, and then your breasts. I want you to tease your-self, Cassie, so don't touch your nipples yet."

Her breathing quickened over the phone, and I let my hand slide up and down my cock once, unable to resist.

"I'm so wet right now, Alex. I can tell my panties are soaked, and I haven't even done anything." Her words shot to my core, an answering groan falling out of me. A drop of come beaded at my tip, and I watched as it slipped down.

"Pinch your nipples, filthy girl. I want to hear you cry out when you do."

She let out a long, ragged moan, and I felt my dick twitch hard in my grip, more come leaking out.

"Now, keep one hand there and move the other down to your pussy. Slip your hand under those panties of yours and rub your clit in small circles."

"Fuck, Alex..." She was letting out moans with abandon now, and I could no longer keep myself from stroking my cock, letting her sexy as hell noises goad me on.

"Cassie, if I were there, I would eat that tight little pussy until you were shaking in my hands and coming in my mouth. I'd keep eating you until I dragged another orgasm from you, licking up every fucking drop."

"You want to know what my pussy tastes like, Alex?"

"Oh god, baby, do I ever."

There was a slick sound from her end, and then her voice. "It's a little salty, but there's a hint of sweetness right at the end. Not too bad if I say so myself."

My head went hazy. "Did you just taste yourself, Cassandra?"

"I did. Is that bad of me?" Her voice was teasing, playful, and I loved it.

"No, baby, that's very, *very* good of you." Her throaty giggle came through, and I decided to really turn it up a notch. "Cassie, I want to hear you come. Whatever you like to do to make that happen, I want you to do it. I want you to tell me what you're doing."

"And what do I get in return?"

"Other than a fan-fucking-tastic orgasm? I will tell you exactly what I'm doing, too."

She hesitated, but only for a second. "When I'm touching myself, I like to rub my clit with my two middle fingers so I get pressure all around. And..."

She paused to let out another moan, and my heart pounded at the mental image of her naked, back arching for the stranger over the phone.

"Tell me, baby." My voice was deeper than before, and I could feel myself getting to the edge.

"And I like touching myself over my panties. I like the way the rough lace or the silk feels against my clit while I'm rubbing it. It makes me come even faster."

"*Shit,*" I mumbled into the phone. I had to clench the base of my cock hard to stop myself from coming at those words. She said them with a little bit of shyness, like she had never admitted that to someone before. For some reason, that hint of innocence drove me crazy.

"I'm really close now, Alex. Please tell me what you're doing."

"I'm sitting in an armchair in my room, naked except for a

pair of boxer briefs that I've pushed down to free my rock-hard cock, which I've been stroking since you tasted your pussy on your fingers. You've got me leaking come, and I'm stroking my cock slowly, rubbing that all around, making myself almost as slippery as that pussy."

"Ah, god, Alex." Her moans were getting louder, and I moved my hand faster, wanting to come with her.

"If I were there, Cassie, after I ate that pussy until you begged me to stop, I would push my hard dick inside you while you pulsed, squeezing my every inch as I pounded you hard into your bed, or the floor, or the wall. I wouldn't care where we were, as long as I could feel you come around my cock and hear you scream my name in my ear. Come for me now, baby. Give it to me."

Cassie let out a shout, her words tripping over each other. "I'm coming, holy shit, Alex, *fuck*, I'm coming!"

I gritted my teeth and tightened my grip, only lasting another stroke up my cock before I started to come as well, breathing out her name as I did.

A few minutes went by while we both panted into the phone, catching our breath. When a small laugh came from her end, I let the smile spread across my face. There was something about her laugh that just warmed me right up. I loved hearing it.

"Well," she said with a croaky voice before clearing it and continuing, "that was... something."

"No shit. I came harder just now than I have in years."

"Really?" I heard the pride and hopefulness in her voice, and I could just imagine her cheeks growing pink.

"Yes really. I would ask if you did too, but I already know you did by how loud you yelled my name when you came."

She let out a scoff, and I knew she was rolling her eyes despite the grin on her face. "You're going to knock yourself out with that giant ego of yours."

"Nah, baby, I'd be more likely to knock myself out with my giant co–"

"Oh my god!," she yelled, the laughter in her voice obvious before she hung up on me.

I let out a loud laugh, still chuckling while I pulled up the messaging app for her company.

"Why'd you hang up? I wasn't done talking yet."

It took a minute, but she responded. *"I wasn't going to sit there and listen to you go on about your giant cock!"*

"I would do no such thing! But, since we're on the subject..."

"Good. Night. Alex."

I laughed again, deciding to give her a break. *"Oh all right. Goodnight, filthy Cassie."*

I turned my screen off, paused, then opened the app one last time, already chuckling to myself while I typed.

"Dream of my giant cock, babe."

What? I couldn't resist.

Chapter 8

Celeste

"N o, Travis, that event isn't until next month. This weekend is the District Arts Fundraiser." I raised my voice to yell my response to my boss, clicking through his event calendar on my desktop.

"What the hell? I could've sworn..." Travis' voice trailed off, his words now an incoherent mutter.

I shook my head at my desk outside his open office door, laughing quietly to myself. I'd been here about three weeks, and it wasn't hard to see that not only did Travis benefit from having a competent personal assistant, but he also absolutely needed one. He'd already mixed up a few events, something his old assistant Emma had warned me about. It amused me, and Travis was a good sport about his own confusion.

What wasn't amusing was how I inevitably reverted to my shy, sixteen-year-old self every fucking time Liam was in the same vicinity as me. He probably still thought of me as some weird little sister of his, all while I was lusting for him in soaking panties. God, all the times I touched myself to the thought of him as a teenager flooded back every time he smiled at me with that stupid face of his.

And by stupid, I meant unfairly beautiful.

I sighed aloud, rubbing my fingers across my forehead to try and encourage the impending headache to stay away. Daydreaming wasn't going to do me any good, and I had plenty of work to do before the fundraiser dinner in two days.

"Long day?"

I jerked my head up with a squeak at the familiar voice, looking up and meeting the gaze of the man I'd just been thinking about. There was a half-smirk on his face, watching me carefully while he leaned a hip against the edge of my desk. I could feel the heat flood my cheeks as I cleared my throat to answer.

"Um, not really. Just tired I guess." My voice was soft, causing him to lean in closer to hear me. His familiar scent of pine needles and something smoky filled my nostrils, and I had to fight to keep myself from closing my eyes and breathing it in deeply.

"Had a few late nights recently?" His voice had taken on a slightly rough edge, the sound going straight to my clit. It also picked at something in my memory, but the effort of hiding my desire for him shoved it to the back of my brain.

"You could say that." My voice was now husky, my automatic reaction tinging the words with a kind of sensuality. My heart froze in my chest when Liam's eyes roamed over me still sitting in my chair before coming back to make eye contact. I swear I could feel the intensity ratcheting up a notch between us.

"Celeste?" Travis' voice had both of us jumping back, making me realize just how close we'd gotten in those few minutes. My face burned anew, and I hastily stood from my chair to go see what he wanted. I could feel Liam follow me, and something wicked inside me prompted me to take a glance back.

Just as I did, I noticed Liam's eyes move up quickly to mine. I turned around just as fast, a pleased smile erupting on my face when I realized he'd been staring at my ass. *Maybe I wasn't just a little sister after all*, I thought, excitement filling me. I did my best to wipe the smile off my face before stepping into Travis' office.

"Yes, Travis?" I moved a few steps inside to give Liam plenty of room to come in as well. When I felt his hand brush my hip, I stiffened in surprise. I turned slightly, catching the hint of a smile on his face as he moved past me.

"I see you've dragged the riff-raff with you," Travis joked when he noticed Liam. "I just wanted to see if there was anything you needed from me before the event since I won't be in the office tomorrow. You'll still be able to reach me by phone if necessary, but if there's anything I can do now to help I've got time."

I ran through things in my mind quickly, going over the list of last-minute to-dos. "I do have one question— what are my responsibilities during the dinner? I know what I'm doing for set-up and take-down, but I'm not sure what I'm supposed to do during the event."

"Oh, I haven't told you? I have people behind the scenes already taking care of everything, so you don't have to worry about any of that. All you need to do is show up and enjoy yourself."

Surprise was likely evident on my face. "You want me to attend as a guest?"

"Of course, Celeste. You've already put in a shit ton of work for this, you should be able to enjoy the benefits."

A smile lit up my face, and then faltered at the realization I had nothing even close to appropriate to wear for it. I made good money, but most, if not all, was going to bills and paying off debts. Not even Madison would have something for me to wear this time.

"If it's all the same to you, would it be all right if I were to stay home? If you need me, I'll definitely be there though," I hurriedly added.

I could feel Liam's eyes burning into me, but I refused to look at him. I could see the confusion on Travis' face, but he nodded.

"Yeah, if you'd rather stay home, I understand. Just know if you change your mind, you're welcome to show up at any time."

"Thank you, Travis." I turned to walk out, leaving Liam and Travis to themselves. Some sort of gravitational pull forced my eyes to glance over at Liam, and a shiver stole through me at the look on his face. I couldn't read what it meant, but it thrilled me all the same.

"No, Mads, I told you, I don't have anything to wear to the fundraiser. And before you start offering your wardrobe, you don't either. It's going to be full of rich people who would spot a Chanel rip-off from miles away. There's not a chance I'd blend into that crowd."

"I resent that statement," Madison pouted at me through the phone. I was at the store picking up some snacks for our movie night tonight, and I'd called to ask her what she wanted this time. She was always wanting a different ice cream flavor, but it took her about ten minutes to talk herself through the process of deciding. It was amusing and irritating at the same time, but trying to get her to decide over text was horrendous—hence the phone call.

She'd somehow segued the conversation into asking about

the fundraiser dinner, and I had to explain to her why I was not going.

"Doesn't matter if you do, because it doesn't change the fact I'm not going."

"It just doesn't seem fair," she sighed.

Thoughts of my life filtered through my brain, tugging at my heart with sadness. I was consumed with bills, unable to finish college, my parents were gone, and I had no family. "A lot of things aren't fair," I mumbled mostly to myself.

Another soft sigh sounded through my headphone, this time one of sympathy. "I know, Celeste. I'm sorry."

"It's okay," I said, shaking off the sadness and storing it away for another day. I had amazing friends if nothing else. "All right, I'm about to check out so I will see you at my place in about fifteen minutes?"

Madison easily accepted the change of topic. "Yes, I am leaving now!"

I chuckled as we hung up, grateful to have her in my life. I checked out quickly, getting home in just under ten minutes. I loaded my groceries into my arms, lugging them up to the front door.

I'd barely managed to hang onto the house I'd grown up in, and then lived in with my dad to help him while he was going through chemo. It was hard to have all the memories sometimes, but I was grateful to have my own space. My porch light turned on as I got near, and it shined on something sitting partially hidden under a pillow on the porch swing I had out front. I looked over at it curiously, struggling to get my keys out to unlock the door. I took my groceries inside, plopping them down on the counter.

I didn't bother to put them away before going back out to the porch to figure out what I'd seen. I stepped outside just as Madison's car pulled into my driveway. I absentmindedly waved to her, moving the pillow over to reveal a slim but large rectangular box, wrapped in shiny black paper with a folded note taped on top. I picked it up and weighed it in my hands, surprised to find it lighter than it looked.

"Whatcha got there?" I turned to find Madison behind me, wildly curly hair up in a ponytail and dressed in sweats and a t-shirt, a couple movies sticking out of her purse.

"I have no idea; it was on the swing when I got home."

She raised an eyebrow. "Seems sketchy. What's the note say?"

"I dunno, I haven't gotten to that part yet."

"Well get your cute little booty in the house and let's see what it has to say!"

I snorted, following her into my home. "There's nothing little about my booty."

"But it is cute," she retorted with sass.

"Ugh whatever." I rolled my eyes and took the package into the kitchen where the light was already on. Setting the box on the table, I took the note off and opened it, reading aloud.

'You really should be going to the fundraiser. See you there.'

I looked up at Madison, feeling more confused now than before. Her face showed the same confusion I was feeling, and we stood in silence for a few seconds before she grabbed the note out of my hand. She read it to herself, her lips mouthing the words.

She looked up at me, holding the note out for me to take. "No one even signed it."

"I noticed." I bit my lip and looked at the box. "Should I open it?"

"Fuck it, woman! Go for it. We're only young once!"

I giggled at her words, reaching for the box. I ripped the wrapping off, finding a white box with gold lettering on the top. Tilting the box to the side, I was able to read the glinting words.

I gasped, dropping the box back onto the table when the brand name registered. Madison pushed me out of the way, grabbing the box and tilting it too, a shriek ringing through the kitchen as she read it.

"Alexander McQueen!" She turned her head to look at me, green eyes wide with astonishment and envy. "Please, for the love of God, open this box so I can look at whatever is inside."

She shoved it at me, and I couldn't help but let her excitement affect me. I opened the box and moved back the piece of tissue paper, gasping again at what I found there. Staring up at me from white tissue paper was loads of aqua lace overlaying nude silk and tulle. I tipped the box, mouth open wide, to show Madison.

"Holy shit! That's one of the dresses from his new line!"

"Take it out for me, Mads," I said in a shaky voice.

She reached in reverently, letting the dress flow out of the box as I dropped it. She turned so we could both stare at it, appreciatively silent.

"You have to put this on," she breathed out reverently.

"Fine, help me into it." We moved quickly to my room, turning on the lights. I stripped quickly, not caring about modesty. I grew up with Mads, I had no shame in front of her. She held the dress up for me and I bent forward to slip into it. She pulled it down my body, helping to smooth it down. I unhooked my bra and whipped it off through the top, adjusting my boobs so the dress propped them up, as it was designed. She turned me to face my full-length mirror.

We stared at my reflection, mouths agape with awe. The dress fit like a glove, hugging my curves in all the right places while the spacing of the lace hid my imperfections. The color of the lace matched my eyes perfectly, accentuating them while calling eyes to my curves. The nude shade of the silk and tulle was barely a shade darker than my skin, making it look like the only thing covering me was the lace until the tulle flared out in pleats at my knees.

"Holy. Fucking. Shit. Celeste. You look... I don't even have words for it." I turned in the mirror to inspect every angle, silently agreeing with her. I couldn't have picked a more perfect dress if I'd designed it myself.

"Who would have sent this to me though?" I asked as I came back to reality. "No one buys a stranger a dress worth thousands of dollars, just because."

"Remember the note? It was talking about the fundraiser. So, it had to be someone you work with."

"Hmm." I looked at the dress one more time in the mirror before I motioned for her to help me take it off. "Travis seemed pretty disappointed when I asked not to go."

"See? It was probably just him being nice."

"I don't know, Mads. It doesn't seem like something he would do. Plus, why would he buy me a dress like this?"

"Who cares? Now you have a dress, and no excuse not to go. And when you get there, just remember to thank him for his incredible generosity."

I rolled my eyes, but she was right. Now I basically had to go, at least to show Travis I appreciated the gesture. I mean, who else could have bought the dress for me?

I changed back into pajamas, resolved not to worry about it anymore. After all, I had scary movies to watch and junk food to eat with my best friend tonight. The fundraiser was a problem for tomorrow.

Chapter 9

Liam

"Well? Did she like the dress?"

"I don't know, Mom. She wasn't home so I just dropped it off." I scrubbed my hand over my face, glad I was just talking to her over the phone instead of in person.

I'd asked her for help in picking out a dress for Celeste so she'd be able to go to the fundraiser. In Travis' office I could see she wanted to go, but something was keeping her from it. Knowing her financial position, I'd assumed it was something to do with not having anything to wear. At least, I was hoping it was, because that was something I could fix.

I'd stared at her enough to be able to guess at her size, and I talked to my mom about finding the dress itself. She delighted in fashion so I knew that was something I could trust her with. I didn't even know what the dress looked like since it came to me in the box already. I'd stopped by the old house, where my mom said she was living now, to give it to her.

After not getting a response from ringing the doorbell, I'd

left the box for her on the porch swing, covered so a passerby wouldn't see it, but she would once she got to the door. I was hoping she'd found it, and I was anxious to see her at the event. I hadn't left my name on the note, worried it would keep her from accepting the gift and the invitation. It's not like we had bad blood between us, but it was a tad bit awkward with all the history between us.

Fuck, now that I think about it, there's not even that much history to go on. I was barely in the house for a month after our parents got married, and I rarely saw them after I moved out. Maybe it just feels like there's so much between us because of what I saw before I left, and because of how fucking bad I want her now. I can barely think when I'm around her because all I want to do is bend her over the nearest flat surface and make her come around my cock. Even thinking about the fact she was once my sister doesn't stop the dirty thoughts parading around in my mind, making my dick harden even now.

No, it just makes you that much harder, my brain helpfully adds. I groan out loud, knowing how fucked up that is.

"What's the matter, honey?" My mom's voice jolts me back from my thoughts, reminding me I'm still on the phone with her.

"Uh, nothing. I'm just tired from putting this event together," I quickly lie. "Speaking of which, I have to go get ready."

"What? How long does it take you to get ready? It's like four hours away!"

"Bye, Mom." I hang up before she could start protesting again. I'm well aware it won't take me that long to get ready, but if I was planning on going to be able to keep a clear head, then I needed to get rid of the hard on currently tenting my sweats.

I was feeling what could only be described as disappointment. It was about two hours into the event, and I hadn't caught even a glimpse of Celeste. My nerves were shot by this point. I'd been distracted all night from trying to watch people come in, hoping every new person was her. I'm sure my inattentiveness was obvious, but I didn't give a shit. My disappointment was becoming annoyance with every passing second; and each glass of whiskey I downed probably wasn't helping.

"Dude, are you okay?" Travis came up beside me with a pleasant smile on his face; one that only someone close to him would realize was strained.

I ran my hand through my hair for the millionth time. "Yeah I just... I thought Celeste was going to show up."

He took a drink from his glass, raising an eyebrow and studying me. "I thought she was going to just stay home tonight."

"Ah yes. Well..." I trailed off, trying to decide how much to say.

"Look, Liam, I've known you for years now. I've never seen you like this, not over a woman at least."

"Like what?" I growled the words out, taking another glance around the room. Nothing still.

"Obsessed. Attentive. I see the way you watch her whenever she's in the room."

I could feel myself get red and I turned to him fully. "Is it that bad?"

He chuckled in sympathy. "You've seen me at my worst. Remember Tania?"

A grin split my lips for the first time tonight. "The Disney girl? How could I forget?"

"Damn, you still call her that? She only dressed up as Esmeralda for Halloween once, man."

"Yeah, but it was liked they'd designed the character after her it was so spot-on."

"Can we move on? I'm just trying to prove a point."

"That I've totally lost my mind over Celeste? Yeah right."

"Oh really? Then you wouldn't want to break the hand of any other man who touched her, especially when she looks like that?" He pointed over my shoulder and I whipped around so fucking fast I could hear the wind whistle in my ears.

My eyes went straight to Celeste who had just walked in, wearing a dress that made it impossible not to stare. Before I realized it, I was already striding towards her. I barely registered Travis' laugh behind me as I left him in the dust.

I was just a couple of feet away from her when she turned her face up to mine, and my heart stuttered somewhere in the middle of my chest. Her eyes were bright, perfectly matching the lace on the dress. The parts that weren't covered in lace were in a nude color, making it seem like the only thing she had on was that lace. Instantly, I had a vision of me ripping that dress right off her and tasting every inch she was teasing me with. My cock hardened in my pants, and I was grateful for the longer jacket I had on that hid it.

I stopped right in front of her, hands itching to touch the exposed skin that wisps of her pale blonde hair were brushing. She had it pinned up and the animal in me wanted to watch it tumble down while I fucked her up against a wall.

Celeste cleared her throat, breaking the silence between us. "Hi, Liam."

"Celeste. You look incredible." I loved the way her cheeks flushed at the compliment, a pleased smile on her face.

"Thank you. I'm going to have to find Travis so I can thank him for it."

"He didn't get it for you." My words were rougher than I intended, but I couldn't stop the fierceness from coming out.

Her eyes widened a fraction. "Did you... This was you?"

I nodded, not trusting my words. "I saw how badly you wanted to come when we were talking in Travis' office. I was hoping with the right motivation, you would still show up. Even if it was a couple hours late."

She laughed nervously. "I wasn't sure if I should come. Madison helped me decide."

"Well, thank God for Madison." She flushed deeper at my words. I held back a groan and offered a hand to her. "Would you like to dance?"

She eyed my hand warily. "I probably shouldn't."

"Why?" She looked back up at me and I felt that same tension I always felt between us at moments like this ratchet up. When I spoke again, my words came out deep and sure. "C'mon, Celeste. Dance with me."

She placed her hand in mine and I led the way to the dance floor, turning and pulling her into my arms when I got there. As she pressed against me, I knew without a doubt my thread of control was not only going to snap, but it was also going to disintegrate.

My conversation with Travis from earlier came into my mind. Had I lost my mind over this woman? I slid my hand lower on her back as we moved into a turn, and the way she drew a sharp breath as our bodies molded to each other told me she was as affected as I was. I felt the need for her, the need to taste her skin from her lips to her feet, flood me.

Goddamn, Travis was right. I was a goner and I'd barely even touched her.

Chapter 10

Celeste

My brain and my body were warring with each other. Every time Liam led me into a graceful turn and our bodies pressed fully against each other, my body gained a little ground in the fight. My brain was telling me I was falling into the kind of fantasy I wouldn't be able to come out of in one piece. It told me there was a piece missing to our story, something important. That nagging feeling was the only thing keeping me from completely relaxing in his arms despite the way my body molded to his at every chance.

I felt Liam's hand lightly brush the top of my ass and my body jerked towards his in response, igniting a sound from his throat that made me instantly dripping wet.

"Celeste..." Liam's voice was pleading and demanding at the same time and I couldn't resist him. I looked up into his eyes and saw the same desire I was feeling reflected back at me. Something in my expression must have clued him in to my thoughts, because one second later he was pulling me out the nearest door and into a darkened hallway. I scrambled to keep up, my heart pounding hard.

He opened a door on his right and pulled me in. I stumbled in my heels, falling into his hard body just as he slammed the door shut behind me. He backed me up against it and I drew in a shuddering breath. I tried to find his eyes, but they were nothing more than a glimmer in the darkness. I felt him lean into me and nip an earlobe. A whimper escaped me, and I let my head drop back against the door.

"I'm going to kiss you," he whispered roughly. "If you don't want me to, you need to say something right now."

My silence was all the answer he needed. He placed his hands on my cheeks to hold me still, and suddenly Liam's lips were on mine.

Years of pent-up desire for this man exploded in that moment. I let out a loud moan, my mouth opening under his. He took the invitation and moved his tongue inside, rubbing against my own and just about devouring me on the spot. My hands came up to the edges of his jacket and held on tight, pulling him into me.

He used his hands to tilt my head to the side, deepening the kiss and lighting my body up. If I had known this was what it felt like to be kissed, I might have tried it out sooner. Or maybe it was just because I was kissing Liam. Either way, I knew I was never going to forget my first kiss.

It would probably surprise most people that Celeste Thompson, a woman in her late twenties, had never so much as kissed anyone, much less had sex with them. It would probably surprise them more to find out that Celeste was Cassandra, popular phone sex operator. Hey, just because I hadn't done anything yet didn't mean I was clueless. That what books and the internet were for, after all.

I just hoped Liam couldn't tell how inexperienced I was by the way I kissed. He didn't seem to have any problem with it, judging by the way he shoved a hand into my hair, messing up the style and popping bobby pins out of place. I loved the way he took charge, the way he couldn't seem to help himself from pushing me against the door and pressing his hips against me.

He broke from my lips and I whimpered in protest; a whimper which was silenced when he began to kiss my neck, biting and sucking on it lightly.

"Fuck, Celeste. I can't get enough of you." His voice rumbled across my skin, and my hips rolled into his, pressing against the length of his hard cock trapped behind his suit pants.

"Liam," I moaned out loudly when he bit down harder on my neck, surely leaving a mark I'd enjoy looking at in the morning.

"Is your pussy wet for me, Celeste? Are you a dirty girl, getting soaking wet for your stepbrother?" His words pinged around in my brain, and I couldn't help the way my pussy clenched hard at his words. It was so wrong to love the indecent way he talked about being related, even unofficially and in the past... But love it I did.

The way I shuddered in his arms must have clued him in to how much I liked it, because he chuckled even as he pulled away from my neck to look at me. One of his hands bunched up in the skirt of my dress as he continued talking, his eyes holding mine prisoner.

"Oh you like that, don't you? You fucking love the way I talk dirty to you, you love your *stepbrother* kissing you and leaving marks on you." His hand slipped under the edge of my raised dress, grazing across the skin on my thigh, getting ever closer to where I throbbed for him. "Tell me, Celeste."

"Yes," I gasped in answer as his big, hot hand found my bare slit, freezing as he comprehended the fact I hadn't worn panties with my dress.

"You really are a naughty, dirty girl, aren't you? You

showed up in a dress meant to tempt and seduce every man in sight, and you wore it without anything else underneath." I let out a choked cry as his fingers delved into my wetness, stroking my clit and then moving to my opening, gathering my juices and pushing a finger inside.

"Oh shit, Liam, that's s-so good." I panted heavily, the sting of something entering my body for the first time mixing with the pleasure I felt swirling in every part of my body.

"That's it, baby, let me make you feel good. I'm going to make you come so hard, my filthy Celeste. Give it to me." My eyes widened, the phrase and tone of his voice pushing the missing puzzle piece in my brain into place. I froze for only a split second, his mouth landing on mine and devouring me again while the heel of his palm rubbed against my clit and his finger continued to press in and out of my hole, teasing a spot on the wall of my pussy that had me shaking with the promise of an orgasm like none I'd ever had.

Everything else was wiped out of my brain in the next second, everything in me going white-hot and screaming into Liam's mouth as I came around his hand. He worked me through it, drawing it out and only slowing down when I began to relax against him. He pulled his finger out of my pussy, letting my dress fall while he licked my juices off his hand. I bit my lip, desire flaring inside me again as I watched the way he cleaned every drop, low groans escaping him and telling me just how much he loved it.

Slowly, the realization from before came back to me, and I stiffened. He noticed right away, and a touch of concern filled his face.

"Are you okay, Celeste?"

I pushed against his chest, making him stumble back in surprise. I reached blindly for the doorknob, heart beating wildly in my chest as I tried to escape.

"Celeste, what the fuck is wrong?" I felt him come up

behind me at the same time I managed to get the handle turned. Flinging the door open, I threw a panicked glance back at Liam.

"I'm so sorry, I just– I have to go." I called the words out as I ran from Liam, ignoring the way he called my name. I disappeared out a side door, not wanting to deal with any of the people at the event in this state. I fumbled for my keys, unlocking the doors and getting in, starting the car and speeding away to my house. I was shaking, one thing repeating itself over and over in my head in Liam's smoky voice.

"I'm going to make you come so hard, my filthy Celeste."

Those were the words that made me realize I was in deeper shit than I'd ever realized. A half-crazed laugh tumbled from my lips, then another, until I was full blown laughing hysterically in my car at my shitty luck. Frustrated tears built behind my eyes and spilled down my cheeks, wondering how I was going to handle all of this when I saw Liam next.

How was I supposed to handle the knowledge that Liam, my stepbrother whom I'd lusted after for over a decade and whom I just gave my first kiss to, and my first orgasm with another person to, was the very same Alex that I'd been talking to as Cassandra?

Liam Alexander Whiscombe. It made sense. And there was no mistaking the way he sounded when he called me filthy, both as Cassie and Celeste. The way he demanded I come for him. My nipples tightened again, my pussy clenching with the memory of his voice and magic fingers.

I shook my head, trying to clear my brain from the way he made me feel. Finally getting home, I parked my car and leaned my forehead against the steering wheel, trying to calm down before I went inside.

The good news was, I suddenly realized, he had no idea who I really was. As far as I knew at least, he didn't know that

Celeste and Cassandra were the same person. And I planned on keeping it that way.

Resolved, glad to have a plan for now I got out of my car and headed inside. I was ready to sleep and just put this whole thing behind me. What was done was done, and I'd just have to keep my distance from Liam in real life from now on. Cassie could have him, but Celeste wouldn't survive the fallout.

Chapter 11

Liam

I tipped back my glass, draining the last of the alcohol in it. It burned my throat on the way down, and I relished the sting. I'd lost count of which glass that was, but I was trying to drown out just how much I'd fucked up tonight.

After Celeste had run away from me, it'd really hit just what had happened. Her addictive scent lingered in the air and on my hand, and even though I'd already started to feel like shit for pushing her too much, I hadn't been able to resist licking her juices off my fingers.

Her taste and sounds lingered even now hours later, the alcohol doing nothing to burn away the memories. My head fell back against my chair, a loud groan leaving my body. I was still hard as a rock, and I knew there was nothing that would get rid of it if I didn't jerk it out. Something in me protested at that, not wanting it to just be me, my hand, and the memories.

It was ridiculous how consumed I was with Celeste. I knew that, but that did nothing to stop it.

She seemed to enjoy herself, the whiskey-drunk voice in my head whispered.

"Yeah, until she ran from me in horror," I muttered out loud. I couldn't stop my mind from going over every detail of the night, how soft and warm and wet she felt, how she made me lose my mind. I could've sworn she was feeling the same things as me, but I just didn't know now.

The only thing I did know was I was never going to be able to sleep with my dick harder than steel. I pulled out my phone, fumbling with it as I made what was, probably, another bad decision.

If I couldn't have the stepsister I wanted so badly, I would focus on the next best thing in my life. Hitting the dial button, I struggled to my feet, heading up to my room. It was still ringing by the time I fell onto my bed, and I wondered if Cassie was even up to answer my call. I was about to hang up when a sleep-roughened voice answered.

"Hello?"

"Uh, hi, Cassie. Did I wake you up?"

There was a pause, long enough to make me think she'd fallen back asleep. Then I heard sheets rustling, and Cassie spoke again.

"Yeah, but that's all right. Are you okay?"

"I'm not sure to be honest." A weird laugh left me, and I realized my words were slurred. What sounded like a normal sentence to me was more like "I'm nit shure, tube honesht" in reality.

"Are you drunk dialing me?" Her voice held a small bit of amusement.

"Maybe. I like yer voice. Makes me feel all warm and shtuff." Her small laugh sounded through the phone, and an answering grin filled my face. Damn, I was more drunk than I'd thought.

"Oh it does? Well I like your voice too, so that works out."

"It does, doesn't it? It. It. That 't' sound is weird, don't you think? It's so loud." I was rambling, but she was laughing so I wasn't going to worry about it.

"You're funny when you're drunk."

"Sometimes. Now I am, before I wasn't so much."

"Hmm? What were you before you called me?"

"Fustraton. Firstrated. Goddamnit," I mumbled into the phone. I couldn't get my mouth to work the way I wanted.

"Frustrated?" Cassie helpfully supplied the word I was looking for, and I snapped in the air, making my body bounce slightly on my bed.

"That's the one! Thank God one of us is sober."

"No kidding. So, Alex, why were you frustrated?"

"Uh, well, I've been a little obsessed with someone I shouldn't be. And I might have fucked up pretty badly earlier tonight. Hence, the drinking." I drew out the last word dramatically, then waited to hear her response.

"Do you want to tell me what you did?" There was a note in her voice I couldn't define, and I wasn't sure if that was because of the alcohol or not. I debated about whether I should tell her, but I figured it wouldn't hurt to give general details.

"There's this girl I knew a long time ago, and now she works in my office. It's possible that I'm a tad obsessed with her, but I fucked things up. Not that I should want her anyway." I let out a huge sigh, then continued, "Every single thing about her is fucking tempting, but I'm trying to control myself around her."

"And your self-control lost tonight." Cassie's sentence was a statement, not a question. She apparently knew where I was going with the story.

"My self-control was obliterated. I've never seen anyone as beautiful as her. And the way she smelled, and tasted... Fuck, Cassie, I can still taste her on my tongue even after the five or so glasses of whiskey I downed after she ran away from me."

I heard her sharp intake of breath at my words, and wondered which part surprised her. Another thought came to mind suddenly, and I voiced it with an apology in my voice.

"Sorry, it's probably rude of me to talk about her while I'm talking to you."

"It's all right, Alex. I don't mind. You just talk about her like she's special to you."

"She is. I doubt she feels the same way after tonight though."

She grumbled something I couldn't catch, and I was about to ask her what she was saying before a yawn interrupted me.

"You should probably sleep this all off. And I doubt it's as bad as you think. Just see how she reacts next time you see her and go with it."

"You're probably right. That's pretty much all I'd be able to do right now anyway."

"Exactly. It's time to hang up now. Good night, Alex."

"Good night, Cassandra." I hung up and let the phone fall onto the bed next to me. I thought I'd be able to pass out quickly, but I lay awake staring at the ceiling for a while thinking about Celeste. Thinking about Cassandra. My alcohol-soaked brain was trying to tell me something, but I just couldn't figure it out.

When I finally started to drift off to sleep, the only thing I could see was Celeste's face right before she took off from the gala. And even though I hated the way she left, I had absolutely no regrets. That was my last thought before I passed out into a restless sleep.

Chapter 12

Liam

Unsurprisingly, things between Celeste and me were awkward– more so than usual. Going back into the office on Monday, I'd been fully prepared to receive a lecture from her, but I should've known that wasn't her style. Instead, I got zero eye contact and plenty of blushing. She ran out of a room every time I entered it, mumbling some kind of excuse for her exit.

It was Thursday now, and I was at my breaking point. I couldn't take much more of this, all my attempts to corner her to clear the air were thwarted in some way. I knew I was going to have to resort to a more underhanded tactic. I was sitting in my office, listening to Celeste and Noelle chatting just outside my closed office door when the idea hit me. I picked up my phone and dialed Travis' extension.

"What's up, man?"

"I need a favor."

I heard him move around, and his voice changed a bit in reaction to my own hurried one. "Sure, anything."

"I need you to borrow Noelle, take her out of the office for something."

There was a pause on his end. "Take her out of the office for what, exactly?"

"I don't care, make something up if you have to. I just need you to take her, and ask Celeste to help me out for the rest of the day."

"Okay..." He drew out the word, obviously confused.

I scrubbed my hand over my face in frustration, not wanting to explain to him what was going on. I didn't want to embarrass Celeste, and I figured having her boss know she'd been kissing the other boss would mortify her. I blew out a breath, knowing I'd have to give my best friend *something*.

"I was a fucking idiot, and I need to get Celeste alone to apologize but she's been avoiding me. This is a last resort."

I heard him try to cover up a snort of laughter.

"Laugh it up, asshole, you still have to figure out what you're going to do with Noelle."

He sobered up quickly, and something about the silence was charged. Suspicion tickled at the back of my brain, but I had more to worry about than whatever was going on between my assistant and my best friend.

"Yeah yeah, just give me a minute."

"Thanks, seriously. I owe you one," I said with relief. I heard him mumbling something, but I didn't stay on the line to try and figure it out. I waited in my office, tapping my fingers on my desk in impatience. Now that I knew I was close to my goal, I was more impatient than before. I sat up straight in my chair and perked my ears when I heard Travis' voice just beyond my door.

"Ladies! You're both looking lovely today."

"Cut it, smart guy, what do you want?" Noelle was a sassy one, and I'd been dealing with her underhanded remarks all week. I'd been afraid that Celeste had spilled the beans, but I knew if she had told Noelle I'd be getting a lot more than odd looks and snarky comments. Obviously, she knew I'd done something to upset Celeste, whom she'd apparently taken to right away, and she wasn't afraid to let me know.

"Down kitty, you can put your claws away. I need your help to go look at a new artist today."

I grinned to myself, knowing I'd be getting Travis a giant gift for this one. He hated going to see new artists, thought they were crazy even though the art was amazing. Noelle on the other hand, adored the process.

As in, she took hours talking to the artist about their works. That was one reason we'd hired her– her incredible passion for art and the people who created it. I usually went with her though, and I was sure she knew something was up.

"Interesting. You know I can't resist that kind of offer though, so I'm in! What's Liam going to do though?"

"Hey, Liam!" Travis shouted through my door, and I pasted on a neutral face before I walked over to it and opened it up.

"God, you could've just knocked. I can hear you plenty fine out here." I leaned against my doorway, fighting the urge to stare at Celeste. My body thrummed with awareness of her, and I itched to get her in my arms again despite knowing how stupid it would be.

"Yeah, whatever. I'm taking Noelle to check out a new artist since you're bogged down with work here. You cool with borrowing Celeste for the day?"

I had to stifle the laugh that wanted to bust out of me in triumph. Travis could be a pain in my ass, but he was a sneaky motherfucker.

"Yeah, that's not a problem. Have a great time out there," I couldn't help but comment. I had to turn away at the glare he threw my way in order not to give in to the laughter.

I went and sat at my desk, listening avidly to the sounds of

Travis and Noelle leaving. I pretended like I was completely focused on my work, but the moment Celeste stepped into my office all my focus was on her.

She cleared her throat softly, and I slowly turned my head to look at her. Fuck, she was beautiful. My cock began to harden in my pants just looking at her, at the way her dress hugged her tits and floated softly around her hips and thighs. She bit her lip, flushing at my intense stare, and I shook myself to snap out of it.

"Celeste, please take a seat," I said in an emotionless voice. I watched as she shifted on her feet for a moment, then walked over to one of my chairs and sat. She wasn't looking at me, and her face was bright red. I hated to make her feel uncomfortable, but I didn't know how to fix it any other way.

"I'm not going to need much from you today," I started off gently, "probably just some copies and sending some emails since I'm pretty hopeless with technology."

She'd seemed to relax when I started off with work instead of referring to the moment from last week where she'd let me kiss her and make her come on my fingers. She even let out a small giggle at my self-depreciating comment. It was true, and everyone in the office knew it. I could never seem to get technology to work for me, and I'd even almost gone *Office Space* on one of the printers once.

"Doesn't sound too difficult," she commented wryly.

"For you maybe," I muttered, loving the small laugh that escaped her. "I can forward you all the information, so let me just help you load the right paper into the copier."

"Okay," she said softly. She stood at the same time, and I ushered her out of my office down to the supply closet. Not able to help myself, I placed my hand lightly at the small of her back. She stiffened momentarily, and I almost pulled my hand away before I felt her relax under my palm.

Satisfaction at that small win roared inside me, and I never wanted this walk to end. I'd never been this affected by one small touch before, and I couldn't believe it was with this woman, one who was off limits for so many reasons.

The supply closet was a fairly large room since it not only shelved our general office supplies, but easels and other hardware we used for displaying artwork at events in our showroom. I let her walk in before me, then led the way over to the specific printing paper I needed for the project I was giving her.

"I'll help you carry the reams, but these are the ones I need."

"Okay, perfect. How many will we need?"

"Three or four." I looked over to my left, and the smile she gave me as she glanced over at me froze me in my shoes. Suddenly, all I could see was her spread out under me, that smile on her face as she came down from one of the many orgasms I constantly thought about giving her.

She must have felt the difference in the air, because I watched her cheeks turn pink even as her back stiffened.

"Celeste, I–"

"Please, don't worry about it." Her words interrupted me, and I was startled into silence. "I know I've been avoiding you, and I'm sorry, but I just couldn't take hearing from you how big a mistake it was, or that you were sorry. And don't pretend like you weren't going to apologize, I could see it written all over your face every time I ran away from you."

"I'm not sorry," I growled. Her eyes widened with surprise. "I mean, I am sorry for making you uncomfortable or making you feel like I was using you. But kissing you was *not* a mistake."

My brain warred with me, arguing that that was exactly what it was. But I didn't care at that point. I couldn't take the hurt and disappointment that had laced her voice, and my anger at anyone who had ever made her feel that way had risen to the surface in a split second.

I stepped towards her, causing her to take a step back automatically. Fortunately for me, there was a wall of shelves behind her, stopping her in her tracks. Crowding against her but keeping a thin breath of air between our bodies, I leaned down closer. Her scent filled my nose, and my cock was rock hard in an instant. I watched her eyes dilate as I got closer, her tongue coming out to lick her bottom lip unconsciously.

"Kissing you was the only thing in my life that makes sense right now, and I just can't seem to help myself when I'm around you."

I watched her mind working and saw it in her eyes when she came to her decision.

"Then kiss me again and prove it."

Her challenge was all I needed. Grabbing two handfuls of her long wavy hair, I held her in place as my mouth descended on hers. I could taste her answering moan, and it sent me into a frenzy. Her arms came around me, nails digging into my back through my shirt as I pressed my body flush against hers.

She pulled away from my hungry kiss and gasped for air, letting out another delicious moan when I began kissing a path down her neck.

"Liam..."

She gasped my name and then ended with a moan when I nipped at the skin between her shoulder and neck, laving it with my tongue to soothe the sting after.

"God, Celeste, I can't get enough of you. I don't know what it is, but I need you more than anything."

"Just don't stop," she replied on a cry. Her hands buried themselves in my hair, holding on and sending sharp tingles across my scalp that only served to make the blood rushing through me burn even hotter.

My hands found their way under her dress, and I moved

them up her exposed thighs to her ass, finding only a small string of fabric nestled between her cheeks, leaving plenty of silky skin for me to find. I pulled away from her neck to look her in the eye, loving the blush that spread on her face as I squeezed her ass.

"Did you wear this tiny little thong in hopes I would find it? Or do you just love being naughty and looking innocent? Is my little stepsister a bad little girl?"

Her eyes widened and her mouth dropped open, hands loosening in my hair. "Don't— you can't say that!"

I grinned wickedly. "Which part, *stepsister?*"

She gasped indignantly. "That part! We're not even related anymore!"

"So, you're telling me it doesn't make you wet when I call you that? You're saying that you'd never think of your step-brother like that?" Her mouth snapped shut and her cheeks turned so red I thought she was going to burst. I knew she was thinking about the fact she'd masturbated to the thought of me years ago, and even though she had no idea I knew, it was fun to watch her squirm.

"I think you like it, despite your protests," I said and moved a hand from her ass to the wet lips of her pussy. Rubbing two fingers across her, I watched as her eyes hooded and her head fell back. I slowly pushed two fingers inside her pussy, gritting my teeth to control myself when her walls squeezed tight around me.

"I... don't... like it," she panted out as I began to thrust my fingers in and out of her, pressing along her front wall as I did and making her tremble in my arms.

My laugh was dark, knowing. "That's because you fucking love, it, *sis*." Her pussy clenched hard around my two fingers, and not even she could stop the moan that flew out of her mouth at my words. "You *love* it filthy, because that's what you are under those pretty dresses and angel eyes."

"No, I'm not." Her voice was needy, telling me she was only protesting because she was stubborn.

"Don't fight it, baby, just tell me how dirty you are."

"How can I be—" she panted then paused, letting out another delicious sound as I pressed my hard cock into her stomach so she could feel me too. "I've never even... oh my *god.*"

She ended on a loud cry when I suddenly took my other hand and pulled the top of her dress down, including her bra, and took her tight nipple into my mouth to suck on it.

I was so hard I thought I was going to come in my pants just from having her tit in my mouth and my fingers in her pussy. Her skin tasted like salted vanilla, and I wanted to eat her up, mark her until she admitted what I already knew.

Through the haze of desire, her previous words finally registered. My fingers paused, my mouth reluctantly left her nipple hard and wet. I waited until she met my eyes and asked the question that burned in my brain.

"You've never even what?"

She bit her lip and looked down. I wasn't having that; I knew that whatever she was going to say was important, and a tingle in the back of my brain told me I already knew what it was. I wanted to hear her say it. I slipped my hand from her pussy and got on my knees in front of her so she was now looking down at me.

Her body trembled, and a hard shiver went through her when our eyes met and held. I began to pull her tiny thong down around her hips and legs, and stated my question again, this time with more command.

"Tell me, Celeste. What have you never done?" I had her step out of her panties and I shoved them into my pocket before she answered.

"This," she whispered. "Any of it."

I felt my cock throb in my pants, and I let out a groan.

"Are you a virgin, little sister?" I pushed her skirt up to her waist, and she automatically went to hold it for me as she nodded shakily.

"Yes," she whimpered as I used my fingers to spread her lips so I could see just how wet she was.

"My little stepsister, such a *filthy virgin*." I leaned forward as I growled the words out, and in the next instant my mouth was on her pussy. She cried out on a strangled moan, and that one sound broke the rest of my restraint. I grabbed her legs and placed them over my shoulders one at a time, bracing her against the shelves as she opened for my lips and tongue to eat her like she was the only thing I needed to survive.

Her salty sweet taste flooded my mouth as her sounds filled my ears, and every lick I made inside her pussy and every flick of her clit only made me want more.

"Oh, fuck, Liam, that feels so good."

Her voice was raspy, and her hands clenched in my hair once again. My pulse beat hard in my body, and I wrapped an arm around her back to hold her as I used my other to reach down and free my cock from my pants. I groaned into her cunt as my dick popped out and I wrapped a hand around it, squeezing the base to keep myself from coming as more of her wetness flooded my mouth.

I jerked my cock as I ate her, my movements making her bounce slightly on my face. I licked my way up from her pussy to her clit, rubbing her little button hard and causing her thighs to shake around my ears. I pulled away for just a moment, just long enough to tell her exactly what I wanted.

"Come for me, Celeste. Come all over your stepbrother's mouth like the dirty, filthy little virgin you are." I dove back into her warmth, wrapping my lips around her clit and sucking, flicking my tongue over her clit in my mouth and sending her screaming over the edge.

I groaned into her, vibrating her pussy and trying to get all the juices that dripped from her pussy as she came, knowing I was about to follow her into that oblivion. She was still shaking from the force of her orgasm as she shifted on my shoulders, pushing herself off until she was standing on her feet again, staring down at me as I fisted my cock. She fell to her knees around me, her thighs straddling mine and putting her bare pussy right in direct line of my throbbing cock.

"Come on me," she said in a hoarse voice. "I want to know what it feels like."

Her naughty words filled my head, and there was no part of me that wanted to deny her.

"Have you ever seen a man come?" I growled the words out, pumping my cock faster as she continued to stare down at it in fascination.

"No, never." Her gaze and words had precum leaking from my tip like a faucet, and I watched as she took a finger to grab some and bring it to her mouth.

"Jesus," I muttered at the sight.

"You taste good," she said in wonder. That was it for me; I moaned loudly as I began to come, shooting my seed all over her bared pussy and tummy, covering her with my load.

The sight was so erotic, I thought I was going to come all over again. Knowing that my stepsister was a virgin, but liked the way I tasted and wanted me to come on her, knowing the way she tasted and sounded when she came... She had no idea, but Celeste was going to be *mine*, just as much as I was already hers.

Chapter 13

Celeste

So much for keeping my distance.

Not only had I decidedly *not* stayed away from Liam, but I'd also spilled the beans about being a virgin and had nearly begged him to relieve me of that status right there in the supply closet.

I groaned out loud to myself, lying on my bed and going over the events of the day for the hundredth time. After Liam had come all over my stomach and pussy, he'd wiped some of it up with his fingers, making me lick it off and sending hot need roaring through me all over again.

He'd been the one to pull back this time, setting me down on unsteady feet and swearing under his breath as he'd tucked his still partially hard cock back in his pants. He'd helped me right my clothes over the mess he'd left, telling me he wanted me to keep him on my skin until I got home; where he'd told me to go after we were both presentable. I hadn't argued, just nodded quietly as streams of guilt and annoyance at myself flowed through me.

Despite my mixed feelings... I hadn't showered. The dirty part of me *liked* having his cum on me. I *liked* the feeling of ownership it left, knowing I'd made him come undone and that he was probably replaying everything in his head hours later just like I was.

My phone lit up with a notification and I opened it up to see a request from the very same man I'd been thinking about. Sort of– technically it was from Alex but since I knew they were the same person it didn't really matter. I bit my lip, trying to decide whether I should take the call.

The wetness gathering between my thighs said I absolutely should. But my brain said under no circumstances should I be taking that call tonight. And my heart... well, my heart was undecided. I struggled with the decision for a couple of minutes, before concluding it would probably be a bad idea in the end.

Sorry, not feeling well tonight. Raincheck? I sent the message, a kernel of guilt lodging in my chest at the lie.

Of course. Feel better, Cassie. His reply came quickly and ended with a little kiss emoji, making me smile despite my turmoil.

What the hell was I going to do?

I still hadn't figured it out days later, and now I was having mixed drinks about my feelings.

Madison, Luke, and Anthony were over at my place for our monthly get-together. It was my turn to host, and I was doing an awful job of it. I'd drunk too much, and everything that had been building with the Liam/Alex situation had only added fuel to the fire of my frustration on top of the three late notices I had gotten in the mail from various collectors.

"I *know* it's fuckin' late, you don't gotta tell me," I grumbled to myself under my breath as I mixed the batter for the cookies I was going to bake. "And he has no right to be so tempting."

"What are you talking to yourself about over there?" Anthony's voice startled me and I whipped around, the chocolate chip dough covered spoon brandished in his direction. It was embarrassingly non-threatening, seeing as how I wobbled on my feet and nearly dropped everything in my hands trying to steady myself on the counter.

"Whoa, girl, it's just me." Anthony laughed while moving to help me straighten up. "No need to attack."

I snorted at him, glaring as I shoved the bowl and spoon at him. "Hush. Now mix. Put those muscles to work for once."

He chuckled but began to stir for me. I watched in appreciation as his arm muscles flexed, but there was no heat to my observation. Anthony was over six feet of deliciousness, with wavy brown hair and hazel eyes that held flecks of 24-karat gold in them, and was built like a football player. It was obvious he was good looking, but nothing about him attracted me. Madison and Luke had tried to set the two of us up in the past, but neither of us had been into it. My lady bits withered at the thought of kissing him, unlike an unnamed forbidden temptation I refused to think about.

"Is it just me, or is something off about Mads and Luke?" Anthony's quiet question had me coming back to the present, realizing he'd been slowly mixing the batter in the minutes of silence while my mind had drifted.

I bit my lip, not wanting to voice my thoughts on the subject. Anthony looked up and met my eyes, and I saw the worry for his brother and our friend that reflected mine.

"I didn't want to say anything, but I've been wondering the same thing. Madison hasn't said anything to me."

"Luke either. He usually tells me stuff, but I asked him the other day and he just ignored the question." He blew a huff of air out of his mouth that made the hair on his forehead lift a bit before settling back down. "It's not like it's awkward between us all or anything either, they're just..."

"Too polite." I picked up where he'd trailed off, thinking the exact same thing.

"That's it. Like when people don't know what to say to each other."

Silence fell between us again, both of us worried for two of the most important people in our lives. Madison and Luke had fallen in love the first moment they met in high school, and had gotten married, living the kind of lives people dreamt about. If they couldn't make it, who could?

"Where are those cookies at?" Madison's voice proceeded her entrance into the kitchen, and Anthony and I hastily tried to look like we hadn't just been talking about her.

Which meant we looked super suspicious, of course. Madison took one look at us and narrowed her eyes.

"What's going on in here?"

I opened my mouth to reply, but I hesitated a second too long and Anthony beat me to it.

"Celeste was just telling me about this man she was muttering about."

I shot him a glare, barely keeping myself from shouting 'liar!' at him in anger. This was *not* a good change of subject! The pleading and sheepish look in Anthony's eyes was the only thing that made me clamp my mouth shut.

"Ooh, are we talking about your hot ex-stepbrother-slash-boss?"

My eyes widened at Madison, the heat rushing to my cheeks as I looked back and forth between her big mouth and Anthony's raised eyebrows.

"What's that?" Luke found his way into the kitchen at the end of Madison's question.

I bit back a groan and closed my eyes, praying to whatever

deity existed to save me from this conversation. Even drunk, it wasn't something I wanted to think about.

"Celeste wants to bang her stepbrother. Who is also her boss," Anthony supplied the not-so-helpful information, and Luke choked on the swallow of beer he'd just taken.

Madison giggled and patted him on the back, helping him choke out a startled, "What?"

"Okay, stop right there, all three of you. He's not my stepbrother—"

"But he was!" Madison cut in.

"*And,*" I said louder to emphasize my point, "he's not my boss!"

"Unofficially though, he sort of is," Madison spoke up again.

"I also notice you didn't say anything about not wanting to bang him," Anthony added.

I let out a little scream, stomping my foot like a toddler who wasn't getting her way. "Shut up! God, it's none of your business!"

Luke wiggled his eyebrows at me. "Still not denying it!"

"Ugh, so what! He already—" I cut myself off before I could continue, slapping my hands over my mouth to stop the words. I grabbed the now forgotten bowl of dough out of Anthony's hands, spinning to start spooning them onto the cookie sheet.

"He already what?" A chorus of voices echoed behind me in sync and I ignored them as the rest of that sentence supplied itself in my thoughts.

He already ate me out like he was starving, so it's not like fucking him would be that much worse.

"Nothing. It doesn't matter. Nothing is going to come out of it anyway." I was glad my back was to them, so they couldn't see the flush that covered my face and the way my nipples had puckered at the memory of his mouth on my pussy.

"Wait, is this that guy from years ago that came with the woman your dad married? What was his name... Lester or something?"

I cringed at the name, grossed out that Luke would even suggest that as a name of a guy I'd be interested in. I heard a smacking sound, and just knew Madison had whacked the back of his head for his ribbing.

"Liam," Madison supplied for me when I stayed silent. "His name is Liam, and yes, that's the guy."

"Either way," I continued, "they were only married for six months before separating so it's not like we were even in the same house together very long. He moved out after a month."

Remembering Liam's abrupt departure from years ago, the ache I'd felt then reappeared in my chest. Even though I'd barely even been able to say a word to him at that point, I'd been so disappointed to not have him around. I thought that crush had petered out after a couple of years, and had even quit asking about him and keeping tabs.

The last few weeks had proved that oh so fucking wrong.

"Celeste?" Madison's voice brought me out of the memory, and I turned to find that the boys had left.

"I'm good, I'm just confused."

"What's the big problem? I know there's more going on than what you've said."

I finished placing rolls of cookie dough on the sheet and placed it in the oven before turning back to my friend.

"Well, you know how I have that job as the phone operator?" Starting with that, I spilled the beans about how I'd figured out my Alex was also Liam, and I was torn between what I should do.

"Celeste, you're thinking about this way too much. Just do what makes you happy. Who gives a shit what's 'right' or 'wrong'? If it makes you uncomfortable, then I would say quit the phone thing. It's not your favorite anyway, and with your new job do you really need it?"

"Well, it would help pay off bills quicker..." That was more of an excuse than a reason, and by the raise of her eyebrow, Mads was well aware of that.

"Take a break from the phone thing for a bit then, see how you do. If you really need it, then go ahead and start it up again."

That was a compromise I could handle. I nodded, feeling more sober than I had a few minutes ago. Madison could tell and poured us both drinks. Just as I was swallowing, she threw a question at me.

"All right, now that we've got that part figured out... are you gonna let Liam pop that cherry of yours?"

Alcohol burned my nose as I snorted it up, coughing as Madison laughed at my reaction, patting me on the back.

"You did that on purpose!" I sputtered the words out through the laughter.

"Well, duh."

I finished wiping the liquor off my face, contemplating. Was it really a question though? My skin tingled and my pussy throbbed at the memory of the last few times I'd been alone with Liam. Would I let him take me, be my first?

"Maybe," I muttered the word out loud, but Madison heard it, whooping in excitement and shoving more alcohol into my hands as I grinned and shook my head at her antics.

The question now, was when?

Chapter 14

Liam

Thoughts of Celeste plagued me all weekend. I'd reached out to Cassie to try and get Celeste off my mind, but she'd been unwell. I wasn't upset about that at all, just disappointed. Something about talking to Cassie soothed me, almost in the same way that being around Celeste did. In fact, now that I was comparing them, I realized they were very similar. I leaned back in my chair at my work desk, contemplating their similarities.

They were both very sweet. Surprisingly dirty. My brain zinged through a multitude of others, and my skin began to prickle with an awareness I'd been too blind to acknowledge.

"Hey, Liam? I was looking for Noelle, but I can't find her anywhere." Celeste's voice interrupted my revelation, and I smoothed my features as she lightly knocked on my open door and stepped inside my office.

I looked her up and down, taking in the way her dress perfectly hugged her curves, the small flare of fabric at her hips emphasizing the cinch of her waist while the pale peach color made it look like her skin was glowing. I swallowed hard, barely registering she'd asked me something. She cleared her throat and that was enough to get my thoughts out of the gutter.

"Oh, uh right. Noelle. She had to leave for a family thing."

"Like an emergency? Is she okay?" She was obviously worried, and I was glad to know they'd built a bond of sorts even in the few weeks she'd been here.

"Yeah, it's her niece's graduation ceremony. No need to worry."

"Oh, thank God. Okay, well sorry to bother you."

I stood from my desk quickly, calling out her name. "Wait, what did you need her for?"

She'd turned, smiling neutrally. "I was just going to see if she wanted to go to lunch with me today."

"I'll take you." The words surprised us both; despite the attraction between us and the situations we'd gotten each other into, we'd never actually just... hung out.

"You don't have to do that," she hedged.

"I know. I want to. Maybe we can catch up a bit," I said with a note of humor in my voice. A small snort of laughter escaped her, and unspoken words hung between us which we both ignored. I followed her out of my office and escorted her out to my car in the parking garage. She murmured a thank you when I held the door open for her, and I took in a peek of her thighs as her skirt rode up when she sat down. Determined to keep this on the right side of friendly, I tore my eyes away.

Driving away from the office, the quiet between us was thick but not uncomfortable. She cleared her throat and I glanced at her, noticing a flush on her cheeks and her hands tightly clasped in her lap. My brow furrowed, and I wondered if she was merely pretending to be okay.

On instinct, I reached over and placed my hand on top of hers, a shock running through me at her touch. I heard her quick intake of breath, and I wondered if she felt the same thing.

"Are you okay, Celeste? If you're uncomfortable, we can go back to the office and go our separate ways. I wasn't trying to force you into anything with my invitation."

"Oh, no it's nothing like that, Liam." She paused, then took a deep breath like she was fortifying herself for what she was going to say next. "It's a little weird, to be honest. We barely know each other even though our parents were married, and then we..."

I bit my lip to keep back the groan at the look on her face as we caught each other's eyes for a split second. She was blushing furiously at the memory, but her eyes were full of need and want that she couldn't get rid of. My cock was already starting to perk up, loving the direction of this conversation. I knew I had to steer it a different way before we got ourselves into trouble– *again.*

"How about we start at the beginning then? What's your favorite color? Animal? Drink?"

"Mint green, giraffe, and orange juice." She fired off the answers without hesitation, going along with the simple questions.

"Wow, me too."

She whipped her head around to face me, eyes wide. I had to bite the inside of my cheek so I wouldn't immediately burst into laughter at the expression on her face.

"Wait, really?"

"No," I said and let out the laughter I'd been holding in. She let out a sound of protest and lightly smacked my arm, laughing as she did.

"You seriously almost had me there," she said while shaking her head. "Like I could really believe your favorite color was *mint green.*"

I turned into the lot for the restaurant, still chuckling at my little joke. Damn, I thought I was funny.

"Yeah, that's a bit far-fetched. I don't think I've ever even thought the words 'mint green' until now."

Our conversation paused as I pulled up to the valet and Celeste's door was opened by the attendant standing there. I stepped out of my car as well, watching as the valet gave her an appreciative glance but then averted his eyes politely. I tipped him well for the effort, knowing it wasn't easy to look away from the gorgeous woman. Placing my hand on the small of her back, I escorted her into the restaurant.

Yes, it was fancy as fuck. The type of place you'd need a reservation weeks ahead for. But I'd sold most of the art in the place to the owner, so it wasn't a problem for me. Sinbad, not his real name I was sure, but it's what everyone called him, specifically had a table reserved for me whenever I wanted it. I'd only used it one other time, but the host's eyes gleamed with recognition the moment I said my name.

We were seated at the table in a private corner, our drink orders taken and left to our own devices for the moment before Celeste spoke up.

"All right, spill it. How the hell did we get in here without a problem when I've been wanting to try this place for *months* with no luck?"

I shrugged, a small smile on my face. "I know a guy."

She snorted. "By which you probably mean you own this place. It wouldn't surprise me, seeing as how you're so mysterious and all now."

"Not mysterious," I quipped back just as the waitress returned with our drinks and took our orders, Celeste letting me order for the both of us since she couldn't decide. After she left, I continued where I'd left off, "Just private. However, you're welcome to ask me anything you want. No limits."

An eyebrow raised in surprise, she reached for her lemon water. "Anything?"

I nodded.

She hummed in thought. "What's the biggest regret of your life?"

Well, then. She didn't pull her punches. I contemplated the answer while looking away although I already knew what the answer was. "Honestly? That I didn't get to know your dad better when I had the chance. I was a stupid kid, frustrated with my mom for getting married again, and I didn't stop to think that your dad was one of the good ones." I paused to sigh. "I mean, I knew he was a good guy because he didn't yell or hit or steal from me or my mom. But she'd already been through so many men I assumed it wouldn't last long so I didn't bother to try with him."

I finally looked over at Celeste, seeing tears had gathered in her eyes at my statement. I shifted in my chair, a little uncomfortable at the raw emotion. I cleared my throat and posed my own question. "If you could do anything in the world, what would it be?"

She sniffed and blinked rapidly, gulping down some more water before she answered. Her voice was a little rough from holding back her emotions, but we both ignored it. "I want to be an artist. It's one reason I enjoy this job so much, because even if I don't get to create the art, I can appreciate it. Be involved in the community. It's a good stepping stone."

"Why not just go for it?"

She looked away from me this time. "I was studying art in school, but I haven't been able to finish yet. I want to go back and learn more, figure out where my true strength and passion lies in the art world, but it's on hold for now."

Before I could ask her why she'd had to stop school, our plates of food were brought in by Sinbad himself.

"Liam Alexander Whiscombe! I thought you'd forgotten

all about me! I haven't seen you in forever, but I'm glad you're here now. And with such a beautiful woman, too." He turned the charm on Celeste, and I grinned as she blushed when he took her hand and kissed the top, introducing himself and praising her beauty and grace in French, his native language.

"I have no idea what you said, but I'm sure it was very flattering," she said with an appreciative smile. "So, thank you."

"No mademoiselle, thank you. This gentleman here does me the favor of providing me with art for my restaurants, and I haven't seen him bring anyone such as you into my fine establishment. I'm very happy you have given him a reason to use the table I save for him."

The last part was said with slight disapproval, and I flushed guiltily. Celeste tsked, winking at me before turning back to Sinbad. "I'll have to bring him more often then, won't I? Now, as much as I appreciate all the compliments, I smell something absolutely divine behind you and my mouth is watering for a taste."

I watched Sinbad puff up in pleasure right before my eyes, his face happier than I'd ever seen it. God, this woman was incredible. She knew exactly what to say to get him back on track and compliment him in the same breath.

"Oh la la, you are correct! I have added a few extra things to your order, on the house, for you two to try." He began to explain the foods to us, but I barely heard a word as I watched excitement and happiness play across Celeste's features. I was mesmerized by this woman from the inside out, and I knew if I wasn't careful, I'd fall hard for her. Then again, I thought as Sinbad bid us farewell and left the food to us, would that be so terrible?

"Holy hell, I don't even know how I'm walking right now," Celeste moaned while clutching her stomach. She leaned back against the nearest wall as we entered the office, closing her eyes and breathing. I laughed quietly, knowing how she felt. We'd both eaten way too much, and the wine Sinbad had sent to us that accompanied the food had been smooth and rich, leading us to drink the whole bottle. We hadn't planned on drinking since we were supposed to be going back to work, but neither of us had been able to resist.

"I think I burst something in my stomach getting those last bites of cake in," I agreed.

"Oh God, that cake," she moaned. My cock jumped to attention at the sound, just like it had when she'd done the same thing with every bite of cake. It had been delicious, but I'd mindlessly eaten bite after bite just watching and listening to her enjoy her piece. I'd nearly come around to her side of the table and tasted the cake on her lips. The mental image still swirled in my mind, tempting me to take the taste now, but I held back.

I wanted to kiss her more than anything, but I didn't want to take away from the friendship we'd built at lunch. That'd been the purpose of today, after all. To know each other on more than a physical level. And we'd succeeded, talking about our lives since I left her house until we'd met up again through this job.

Celeste was brilliant, fascinating, self-sacrificing, and she cared a great deal about her friends. Every little piece of information I learned only made me want her more. In my bed, in my life. And if I didn't stop thinking about it now, I was going to take that pouty little mouth with mine right here, in the middle of the open office, for anyone to see.

Her eyes opened and found mine, hazy contentment very similar to what she'd looked like when I'd made her come days ago making me nearly lose control.

"Thank you for lunch, Liam. I really appreciate it."

I smiled back at her. "It's no problem. Thank you for letting me take you."

We stood there smiling at each other in silence, neither of us sure what to do next. We both jumped a little when Travis came from nowhere, his voice ringing out and startling us.

"And where have the two of you been? Getting up to no good, I bet!"

I felt heat rise on my face at the same time Celeste began to blush, despite the lunch having been completely innocent. *Well, mostly,* I thought to myself at the memory of all the times I'd nearly kissed her.

"I took her to lunch as a thank you for helping out so much around here," I supplied casually.

"Mhmm," Travis hummed noncommittally, and I wondered if he knew something was up. I hadn't told him about my slight obsession with Celeste yet, but I had a feeling it wasn't going to stay secret for long. "I'm just messing with you guys, I just barely got back five minutes ago. Go ahead and get settled, Celeste, and then come see me so I can give you an update on the next shipment we're getting."

"I'll be in in a few minutes," Celeste said pleasantly and headed towards her desk to put her stuff down. Travis stayed by me and thankfully waited until Celeste was out of sight to grill me.

"Anything I should be worried about?"

"Not at all. We're just figuring out where we stand, what with our history and all." *And the making out. And touching. And tonguing.* I kept that last part to myself.

"All right. I trust you, but that one's dangerous."

I snorted. "You have no idea." Travis clapped me on the back in sympathy and then headed over to his office. I turned with a mental sigh, heading off to my own. Noelle would be gone for the rest of the day, so I had a few things to cover for her so she wouldn't be behind when she got back. I knew I'd be able to get lost in the work and not over analyze the shit out of what was happening between Celeste and me.

Not to mention the fact that with Celeste's first bite of cake and the following moan, I'd figured out exactly what had been niggling the back of my mind earlier. I'd nearly tossed the idea at the ridiculousness and plain coincidence, but when I'd closed my eyes with Celeste's second moan and listened to her quiet, "Oh my God, that's so good", I'd known it was true.

Cassandra from my late-night phone adventures and my stepsister Celeste were one and the same. What I was going to do with that knowledge, other than ignore my hard-on from the realization, I had no idea. Did I tell her I knew? Did she know who I was? She'd never let on that she had any clue, so maybe she was as oblivious as I had been.

Shaking my head to clear it, I knew this was something to contemplate for another day. I grabbed a stack of folders from Noelle's desk as I passed and lost myself in my work until I had to go home. Something that didn't seem as appealing as it used to, now that I knew I wanted someone there with me. And it was no mystery who that person was.

Chapter 15

Celeste

"And now my nipples get hard every time he comes around! Actually, it's worse than that. All I have to do is hear his voice and my panties are wet like that!" I snapped my fingers to emphasize my point, and Madison cackled.

"It's not funny," I grumbled and shoved a chip loaded with salsa into my mouth. I'd like to say we were drunk, but we weren't. I'd also like to say we were at home where no one could hear about how embarrassing my work life was now, but that would have been a lie as well.

Madison and I were in the corner of a Mexican restaurant on a Thursday night, where I was spilling the beans about my current love life– if you could even call it that.

I'd raised my voice a bit with my dismay, but what else was I supposed to do when just the mere thought of Liam had my breath speeding up and my face flushing? I was turning into a mess. And it was all his fault! If he hadn't taken me out to lunch earlier this week, we wouldn't have had that time to get to know each other. I wouldn't have gotten to appreciate the man for who he was, not just what he made my body feel. My heart was getting involved, and it was fucking with me.

I glared at a couple of guys a few tables away from us who were eavesdropping and glancing over at our table, and they quickly looked away. I turned back to Madison, shoving another chip into my mouth while she continued to laugh at my expense.

"I'm sorry, Celeste. I've just never seen you this put out over a guy before. It's quite entertaining." She burst into another fit of giggles at the glare I gave her.

Thinking about her words, I realized she was right. And I guess I could sort of see the humor in the situation. My lips twitched with a smile, and a snort of laughter escaped me.

"All right, enjoy it while you can. Just wait until I'm crying on your shoulder and eating all your ice cream when my heart is inevitably broken!" I said the words with humor, and although she laughed at my joke, her eyes went dim. "Mads?"

She looked away and grabbed a chip. Now she was the one eating them to avoid dealing with something. I reached over and placed my hand on top of hers. My heart clenched when I saw her bottom lip tremble, and I was worried when she looked up at me and I saw tears begin to spill down her cheeks.

"Oh, Madison," I breathed. I immediately scooted out of my side of the booth and went to hers, wrapping my arms around her so she could quietly cry on my shoulder, just like I'd joked about doing to her a second ago.

Thank God, we were in a corner and there was barely anyone around. I waited a few minutes while Madison cried and then gathered herself together, sniffling and grabbing a napkin to wipe her eyes and nose.

"Madison, tell me what's going on. You can't hide it now." I kept my tone soft but phrased my words so she knew she wouldn't get out of it.

"I'm sorry, I know this was about you and I don't mean to monopolize it with my own problems."

I let out a sound of disbelief, waiting until she looked me in the eyes to respond. "Madison, you are my best friend. There's no 'about me' or 'about you' here. I know you've been holding something back, and I figured you'd tell me about it when you were ready, but now I'm thinking you just didn't want to burden me."

She flushed guiltily and nodded. "Yeah. You've had so much to deal with, and then things started to go so well for you and I didn't want to ruin it for you."

"Well, first of all, that's dumb. I always want you to tell me when you've got something going on. You don't always have to be happy or perfect Mads. You're allowed to break down, to struggle. To be imperfect. Now tell me what's wrong."

I waited patiently while she cleared her throat, trying to put her words together, but when she spoke she dropped a bomb I never would have expected to hear.

"Luke and I are separating."

My jaw dropped in shock, and my blood froze. "What?"

She nodded at my whisper, eyes filling with tears again and voice trembling when she continued, "About six months ago, we found out I was pregnant."

A squawk-like sound left me, interrupting her sentence. They hadn't said anything to anyone!

"Before you get excited, we... lost the baby about three months in. That was the third time," she whispered brokenly. "My third miscarriage. And no matter what we do, we can't seem to make it past three and a half months."

"Oh my god," I murmured. I could feel her heartbreak

like it was my own. I knew she and Luke had wanted to have kids for forever, and to have that chance taken away from them so many times... It would have been devastating.

"We've started to blame each other for it, and we can barely stand to be in the same room together. We've kept up the act in front of everyone, but it's becoming way too hard to keep it up. We talked about it, and we think we need to spend some time apart. Figure out who we are individually instead of as a couple. I mean, we've been together since high school, and never really got to know who we were before getting married."

She let out a deep breath, and I could tell this had been weighing on her for a while. "When did you guys decide to separate?"

"After the last get-together. He said he'd talk to Anthony about staying with him, and that I could stay in the house."

"Well at least it's just separation, not divorce. I'm assuming you guys still love each other?"

"Oh God, Celeste, I still love him so much. I just don't know *how* to love him anymore." A tear fell, and that's when I knew, Thursday or not, we needed that margarita fishbowl stat. I waved over the waiter and ordered one, and he must have realized the desperate need for it because he came back with it in less than two minutes.

"All right, Madison, here's what we're going to do," I said as I moved the drink to the spot between us, giving her one straw and taking the other. "We're going to chug this fishbowl like we've been wandering in the dessert for forty days and forty nights and this is manna from Heaven. Then we're going to get a ride back to my place where we're going to drink some more until we're singing along with 80s music in our underwear. You're going to stay the night and we're both going to call in to work so we can stay hungover in bed all day and not worry about Luke or Liam or real life for at *least* the next forty-eight hours. Deal?"

She gave me a watery smile. "Deal."

Our rendition of Def Leppard was admittedly terrible, but we were having a good time, nonetheless. Taking turns belting out the chorus lines, we were in my kitchen in mismatching bras and underwear, a whisk in her hand and a spatula in mine like they were microphones.

We'd already had a bottle of wine – or two – and several shots of tequila, and we were trashed. True to our deal, we hadn't mentioned anything about our lives since we downed the margarita at the restaurant, instead focusing on having a good time and letting go for a little.

"Oh crap," Madison suddenly muttered. Her face went pale and she dropped the whisk, running to the bathroom just around the corner. I followed her on drunken legs, getting there just in time to help hold her hair back while she tossed her cookies.

"I'm thinking maybe it's time for water and bed," she said after finishing up.

"I think you're right. It's after 3 a.m. anyway. Don't forget to send an email about not coming in. All you have to say is you puked and you're free and clear!"

"Ugh, don't remind me. I'll be happy if I never see that side of your toilet again."

"Well, I'm fairly sure the toilet feels the same way." Giggles burst from me at the joke, and Madison joined in reluctantly. We stumbled out of the bathroom and upstairs to my room with my giant bed. Both of us fell back onto it, not even bothering to climb under the covers.

I was just drifting off from a mix of exhaustion and alcohol when I felt Madison grab my hand. I woke up just enough to hear her quietly whisper her thanks to me.

"Anything for you, Mads," I mumbled before the two of us passed out.

Chapter 16

Celeste

I groaned and squinted my eyes shut, pouring myself another cup of coffee. Yes, it was like 4 p.m., but with a bitch of a hangover like the one I had, it was necessary. Madison had woken up around noon with barely any aftereffects, per usual. I had no idea how she did it. Although it might have something to do with the whole puking-her-guts-out-before-bed thing.

Thankfully, she'd gone around and shut all the blinds in my house and started some coffee before she took off. If it hadn't been for the darkness and the tantalizing smell, I probably never would've gotten out of bed. I'd already refilled the coffee once, and I'd just taken some ibuprofen to get rid of the last of my headache.

A knock sounded on my door just as I took a sip of freshly brewed beans, surprising me and making me take too big of a drink. I cursed as the hot liquid burned my tongue, while making my way towards the door. Peeking through the hole, I was shocked to see Liam standing at my door, a balloon in his hand.

Stepping back from the door in horror, I quickly glanced down at myself, and then up at the mirror on the wall next to me. My hair was a greasy, tangled mess, my makeup was still crusted around my eyes, and I was wearing a stained and ratty t-shirt accompanied by men's boxer shorts with 'Pussy Wagon' written on the ass that Anthony had bought me as a joke from some online store.

"Celeste, I know you're in there. I heard you swear."

I cringed, realizing I'd spoken way too loudly when I'd burned my tongue a minute ago. "Go away, I'm not fit for company."

"I'm not company. I'm your brother; let me in."

I flushed at his words and couldn't help but open the door a crack just to glare at him.

"Step-brother. Ex. Now leave me alone." Before I could slam the door shut Liam pushed his way into my house, nearly losing the balloon he was holding in the process.

"You should know by now I always get what I want," he said in a light tone that, for some reason, had me blushing all over again.

He didn't mean like that, I mentally scolded my perked nipples.

We stood facing each other, and I wanted to smack the little smirk off his handsome face when he took me in.

"Looking good, sis."

"Shut. up." I looked up to the balloon, noticing the 'Get Well!' and my annoyance faltered a bit. "Is that... for me?"

His eyes followed the direction of my pointing finger, and I could swear I saw him blush a little. "Uh, yeah. Travis told me you called in sick, so I thought I might come by to cheer you up a bit."

A weird silence fell between us, neither one of us sure what to do about the gesture. I cleared my throat awkwardly, stepping forward to take it from him.

"Well, thank you, Liam. I appreciate the thought."

He placed the ribbon in my hand, and then took a few loud, curious sniffs. "Why do you smell like week-old tequila and wine?"

I stepped past him quickly to hide the guilt. I could feel him following behind me, and I had never been so grateful that Madison had cleaned up before leaving. I didn't need Liam to know that the reason I'd called in was because I'd been completely wasted at 3 a.m. Despite having a good reason, it wouldn't look good for my job to have called in because of a hangover.

"Celeste?" Liam put his hands on my shoulders and turned me around to face him. I kept my face down, not wanting to admit anything. "Are you... Should I be concerned about your drinking?"

My head shot up to finally look at him, and I burst into laughter at the worry on his face. He thought I was a drunk!

"Oh my god, no, Liam. I'm not an alcoholic. Despite the current evidence. I was comforting a friend last night, and we got a little carried away is all." I'd take that confession over him thinking I needed rehab!

His face cleared, and he stepped back. "Oh, good then."

I bit my lip and watched as his eyes narrowed in on the movement. I suddenly registered the heat sparking between us, and despite feeling disgusting, I wanted him to kiss me so badly I knew I needed to get him out of here.

"Well thanks for stopping by," I said and tried to herd him towards the door.

"Oh, no, you don't. You're not getting rid of me that easily. I have somewhere to take you, so go get showered and ready. Casual clothes are perfectly fine."

"What? I'm not going anywhere," I sputtered.

He stepped closer to me and I flinched, not wanting my smell to horrify him. He didn't seem to care, backing me into the countertop behind me and putting his hands on either side of me to trap me.

"Yes, you are Celeste. I promise you'll like it," he said. I tried to hide the shiver that went through me, but I'm sure he caught it. "Just trust me, and do as you're told." He pulled back and gently pushed me towards my stairs.

"Fine. Don't think you can order me around like this all the time, though!"

"I will when it's needed. You'll get used to it or pay the consequences," he said matter of factly.

I turned and stomped away, only pausing when I heard a choked laugh behind me. Whirling around, I caught the giant grin on his face as his eyes moved up from my ass to look me in the eye.

My ass. My 'Pussy Wagon' shorts had been revealed when I'd turned in a huff, and a new kind of heat filled my face. I decided to ignore him and his amusement with my clothes, so I turned right back around and went up the stairs. I jumped in the shower, letting out a moan at the feeling of the warm water beating down on my skin. I hated that Liam had suggested this, and probably knew how much better it was going to make me feel to clean yesterday and last night off me.

Thirty minutes later, I was heading down my stairs with half-dried hair, a green tank top, and rainbow workout pants. He did say to dress comfy, after all.

"Liam?" I called out his name, wondering where he went.

"Kitchen," he replied, and I headed that way to see him fiddling around with my coffee pot. "You know," he commented without turning to face me, "the wiring on this thing could cause a fire if you're not careful."

He turned to face me, and I watched in fascination as his eyes dilated while they ran down my body from my hair to my toes bared in sandals. I mean, I didn't even put any makeup on and he looked at me like he wanted to throw me on the table and devour me.

I felt my nipples furl under my thin bra, and just knew they were obvious in this top. I did my best to ignore the sexual tension between us and addressed his last comment about the fraying cord to the coffee pot.

"Nothing's happened yet."

He blinked slowly, his darkened eyes coming back up to meet mine. "What?"

I swallowed a pleased laugh. "The wiring. Everything's been fine so far," I squeaked out. This was a new side to him, and I think I liked it.

He seemed to come to a conclusion, and a small frown marred his face. Not that it made him any less handsome. "That doesn't mean something can't happen. You need a new one."

I shifted awkwardly. "I haven't really been able to afford a new one," I mumbled.

He seemed to notice my uneasiness with the turn of conversation, and smoothly changed it. "Well, are you ready to go?"

"As ready as I'll ever be." His answering grin took the breath from my lungs.

"Let's get out of here then," he said and propelled me out the door, making sure I locked it behind us. I squinted in the light, not prepared for the brightness. Digging in my purse for sunglasses, I followed Liam over to his car. When he opened the door for me and helped me inside before going around to his own door, my heart fluttered a bit. No one had ever done that for me before. Liam didn't even have to work hard to worm his way into my heart; all he had to do was be himself.

We rode in his car quietly, the silence between us not uncomfortable at all. Usually I couldn't handle that, but he seemed so content to just be here with me that I didn't mind it. Soft music played in the background and I mouthed along to the words as Liam drove. I couldn't help but glance over at him out of the corner of my eye, watching the way his muscles played under his shirt as he drove. Remembering the way he'd looked at me in the kitchen did nothing to cool my libido, and I was close to squirming in my seat to relieve some of the ache when he spoke up.

"I hope you're hungry."

"I am actually," I said with surprise. Despite feeling horrible this morning, the shower and multiple cups of coffee I'd drunk must've worked their magic. Glancing over at Liam, I mentally acknowledged he might have had something to do with that too.

"Good," he responded with a smile, turning left into a parking lot. I watched as he parked in front of what looked like a run-down diner, and then glanced over at him with raised eyebrows as he parked.

He looked at me after turning the car off, and laughed at my expression of incredulity. I forgot about everything else but the way he looked, head thrown back and eyes crinkling in complete happiness. His laughter filled the car, and it was so contagious I was soon giggling along with him.

"Oh man, that's one of my favorite parts about bringing people here." He was talking about the diner, which was simply named 'FOOD'. No, it wasn't sketchy at all.

"You like bringing people to a diner named 'FOOD' that looks like it's about to fall apart and watch as they look at you weird?"

He nodded emphatically. "I absolutely do. I know it doesn't look inviting necessarily, but I swear it's safe. This place has the best hangover food, I swear it."

"Okay," I said dragging out the word before opening my

door and stepping out. I followed him into the diner, and I knew my face was covered in shock when we stepped inside.

The outside of the diner might have looked like I should turn and walk the other way, but the inside was obviously well taken care of. Tabletops gleamed, jukebox music played in the air, and I felt like I'd been transported right into the 40s. The place was full of people, but not too many to be overwhelming and we were able to find a corner booth easily enough.

"This is unexpected," were the first words that left my mouth after the waitress had stopped by to drop off menus and take our drink order – large cookies and cream shakes for both of us, something I was very excited about.

He chuckled. "I know. When I first came here, I wasn't prepared. To be honest, I was probably still a little drunk from the night before, so going from the shabby exterior to this," he said gesturing around the restaurant, "made me feel like I'd stepped into an alternate dimension."

"That's almost exactly what it's like! If you looked at an un-restored diner from the 40s, the outside is exactly what it would look like today. But then you come inside, and it's like you traveled back in time. Pretty clever idea, actually."

"I'm glad you can appreciate it. Once I'd figured that out, I knew I'd be coming back every chance I got."

"When did you first come here?"

For some reason, he glanced down at his menu and his cheeks turned pink at my question. Before I could interrogate him about his reaction or wait for an answer, the waitress came back over with our shakes and took our orders.

After ordering what felt like half the menu, we gave them to her and I turned back to Liam, not forgetting my earlier question or his reaction to it.

"Well, Liam? When was your first time?" His eyes twinkled at my question, and I realized too late how it had sounded.

"Ugh, never mind." I didn't need to be teased about my own non-existent first time.

Thankfully, he ignored my blunder. "A couple of days before I moved out of you and your dad's place."

I wondered why he hadn't called it our parents' place, since they'd been married at the time. I shrugged that off though, moving on to my follow-up question.

"And why were you so drunk?" Another thought popped into my head. "How did you even get drunk? Weren't you like eighteen or something?"

He flushed at my questions, avoiding my eyes again before answering.

"I didn't really look just eighteen, I had a pretty good fake ID. I'd never used it before then, and I can't tell you how nervous I was when I tried it." He paused, a small smile twitching at his lips.

"I can imagine. But you ignored my first question."

"I don't remember why I was drunk."

It was a lie. I just knew it, but I didn't want to make things awkward between us by pressing the issue. I figured that was his own business so I let it go, taking a drink of my shake.

A low moan escaped me as the taste hit my tongue, and my eyes closed as I drew more into my mouth. "Holy shit, that's good," I said.

A growling sound had my eyes opening and focusing on Liam, whose expression had turned hungry once again. Heat gathered in my chest – and other places – and I licked my lips to catch a little of the shake that had caught on my mouth. A small groan escaped Liam's own mouth, and my panties were wet in an instant.

I squirmed in my seat, and Liam didn't miss the small shift. Scooting a tad closer, he talked quietly enough for me to be the only one to hear.

"Are you wet right now, Celeste?" I couldn't make myself

answer the question aloud, so I just nodded jerkily. His lips curved into a satisfied smile. "Good, because I'm fucking hard as a rock right now from that moan you let out, and I wanted to make sure I wasn't alone."

With that, he scooted back over to his previous spot at the booth, eyes roaming over me and focusing on my once again peaked nipples. I glanced away and caught sight of our waitress heading our way with our tray of food, and I was more than grateful for the reprieve. She unloaded the plates onto our table, and I closed my eyes in pleasure as the scents drifted up to me.

Bacon, chocolate chip pancakes, eggs, potatoes, and some skillet rightfully dubbed 'The Cure' teased me, and without further ado both Liam and I dug into the food we'd decided to share. I couldn't help the noises I made as I ate, and I just had to ignore the way Liam watched me, the feeling of hunger between us not dissipating in the slightest.

Chapter 17

Liam

Well fuck.

Eloquent, right? But that's all I could think, from the moment Celeste had opened her door looking and smelling like a mess, to this moment right here with her in my car on our way back from the restaurant. Together we'd devoured every bit of food we'd ordered, and I'd been hard the whole goddamn time. All I could imagine was pulling her under the table and having her swallow my cock while she made those delicious sounds around me until I shot my come down her throat.

I'd come over just to check on her, but when I'd realized she'd been suffering from a hangover, I knew exactly what she'd needed. I kept telling myself it wasn't my dick, but that particular appendage was decidedly not in agreement.

I pulled into Celeste's driveway and cleared my head so I could make sure she got into her house safely. I came around to her door to hold it open for her as she stepped out, and then walked alongside her as we made our way up to her door. I took a step in the grass, and it squished underneath my shoe.

Squished? That couldn't be right. It hadn't rained in days, and today itself had been clear. I looked around for signs of sprinklers and noticed the sidewalk at the end of her grass was also wet. Something about this didn't feel right, and I hurried to catch up with Celeste who'd kept walking without me.

"Uh, Celeste?" She turned to me with a question in her eyes as she unlocked the door and opened it. Before I could say anything else, a flood of water ran out the open door and splashed over her toes, making her jump and shriek. Not caring about my own clothes, I quickly moved past her into her home, noting the damage as I tried to find the source of the water leak.

"Oh shit!" Celeste's words were filled with horror as she followed me in. I agreed. The damage was already bad, in just the couple of hours we'd been gone. I noticed water on the stairs leading up to the second floor, so I ran up them, trying not to cringe at the squelching of water under my feet.

I ran into her bathroom and my eyes widened at the scene before me. Her tub was overflowing, the water bubbling from the drain up and over the rim. I could tell this wasn't the source of the problem, merely an outcome. Rushing back down the stairs, I heard some banging coming from the basement.

I went down the flooded stairs, wading through the water and over to where Celeste was trying to reach the spigot to shut her water off. Reaching over her head, I turned it as tightly to the right as possible. We stood there listening as the sound of water speeding through broken pipes calmed, and Celeste turned to me with unshed tears in her eyes.

"Well, at least my house didn't catch on fire," she said in a wobbly voice. A choked laugh flew out of me at the terrible joke, and I gathered her in my arms as she burst into tears.

She cried into my shirt, arms wrapped tight around my waist as I held her, doing my best to comfort her. This was a huge problem, not just for anyone but for Celeste. I'd snooped through the bills I'd accidentally found in a kitchen drawer while she'd been in the shower, and that had made me realize she was worse off than I'd ever thought. If she couldn't afford a new coffee pot, how the fuck was she going to afford to get this fixed?

I could feel Celeste start to calm down, and I let her pull away slightly as she sniffled and wiped her face.

"This is all my fault," she said finally.

"What? How could this be your fault?"

"I'd known something was wrong, but I was too afraid to figure out what it was because of how much it would cost. And now I've made it worse."

"Celeste, listen to me. This was an accident. It's not your fault. I'll call some people and get them over here to start clearing out the water and assess the damage."

"No, I can't let you do that. This is my responsibility; I'll take care of it." She struggled out of my arms, and I managed to grasp her elbow before she could get away from me.

"I want to help. And whether or not you want to admit it, you need my help. So, I'm not going anywhere."

I felt a tremble go through her, and I moved to come around to her front. I put my hand under her chin and tilted it up so I could see her.

"Hey," I said calmly, "we'll get this figured out. Okay?"

She bit her lip and I could see she wanted to argue out of pride, but after a moment she whispered, "Okay."

"Good." I placed a kiss on her forehead and then wrapped her hand in mine as I went back up the stairs, making sure she stayed with me. Thankfully, I'd left my phone in my car, or it would've been ruined by the accidental underground pool in Celeste's basement.

The next two hours were filled with phone calls and people coming in and out of her house, trying to do as much damage control as possible. Celeste had contacted her insurance company, and they were going to be out tomorrow to look at everything. We'd managed to get the water pumped out of her basement, and her tub upstairs had begun to drain the moment we turned the water off. I'm pretty sure it all ran back down into her basement, but it wouldn't have made much of a difference down there.

Now, everything was just soaking wet. And not in a sexy way. I looked around Celeste's waterlogged house, letting out a big sigh. I went in search of Celeste, following the sound of her voice.

"I can't do that, Madison. Yes, I know. Do you know how awkward that would be? For all of us?" Celeste was speaking quietly but firmly, talking to Madison on the phone.

I leaned against the doorway, waiting for her to finish so I wouldn't interrupt her. I felt a little bad for eavesdropping, but with her next words I was glad I had.

"No, I'll just get a hotel room for a little while and go from there. I'm not sure, but I'll figure it out."

"Stay with me." The words left my mouth and made Celeste jump a foot in the air. She whipped around, pressing her hand against her chest and she panted.

"Fuck, you scared me, Liam!" Madison asked her something, and she said into the phone while staring at me, "He's been helping me out here." She paused to listen to Madison again, and I would've given anything to hear what she'd said since Celeste's face went beet red. "Shut it. I'm still not coming over there."

"Stay with me," I repeated. "I have plenty of space, and I swear I'm not the worst roommate."

She cracked a smile at that, and I was relieved to see it. My strong girl was back, and I was glad for it.

"I think I've figured something out, Mads. Thanks for the offer, though. Yes, of course I'll keep you updated. Love you, too." Celeste hung up the phone and then crossed her arms under her breasts, plumping them up and tempting me to take a glance. A temptation I valiantly fought.

"Well, how about it?" She seemed to be thinking over the offer, and I knew I had to press my advantage. I couldn't say why I wanted her to stay with me so badly, but once the idea had popped into my head, I'd known that was exactly what needed to happen.

"Look," I continued, "you can't stay here. You can't afford to stay at a hotel for the unforeseeable future. I have plenty of space, and I'll let you stay for free. What's there to think about?"

Just the idea of having her under the same roof made my blood heat. The more time I spent with her, the harder it was getting, no pun intended, to stay away. I was getting more and more obsessed, thinking about her all the time and replaying what she looked and sounded like when she came, how she tasted. How she laughed, how she cared for others, how stubborn and independent she was.

"If I stay with you," she spoke cautiously, "what exactly would that entail?"

My mouth and fingers on your pussy whenever you wanted. My cock too… if you begged for it. I kept the thoughts to myself, giving her a more diplomatic answer out loud.

"You'd have your own room. Free rein of the kitchen and basically anything else you needed. I'd give you a key so you could come and go freely. Basically, it's like living with a roommate who doesn't need you to pay rent."

"I don't like not paying you anything. I can cook for you, and make sure everything stays clean. I want to feel like I'm exchanging something, not just taking from you."

I pretended to contemplate it, although I already knew I'd

say yes. I wasn't a messy guy, so she wouldn't have much to clean up except for whatever she did. And as far as cooking goes, I was abysmal at it anyway so that was a huge benefit.

"All right, I think I can live with that. Let's get some things packed, and you can follow me to my place."

She moved to her closet and pulled a suitcase down from the top shelf, saying how she was glad she kept it up there. I made a sound of agreement, but my thoughts were once again nowhere near anything clean.

The last time I'd really seen this bedroom, Celeste had been lying on that bed, touching herself and saying my name. Something in me snapped at the memory, and all the tension and heat that had been building between Celeste and me came to a head. Even through taking care of this untimely disaster, I'd felt it. Seen it in her face. I moved closer to her, needing to feel her under my hands more than anything else.

She was standing at a dresser, unloading everything from the drawers that had stayed dry, and I moved up behind her. She looked up into the mirror, staring at me in the reflection as I placed my hands on top of hers, stilling them. She must have seen the hunger in my eyes because a stifled sound of need reached my ears a moment later.

I leaned down, brushing her ear with my lips before I began to speak.

"That question you asked me in the restaurant? About why I was so drunk? I lied when I said I couldn't remember."

"I know."

I raised an eyebrow at her in the mirror, and she shrugged.

"Hmm. Would you like to know what the real answer is?"

"Yes please," she whimpered while I placed a kiss on her neck.

"The reason I got so drunk that night," I confessed as I began to run my hands up her arms until I was cupping her full breasts in my hands, the nipples poking my palms excitedly, "was because I saw something I shouldn't have. And what I saw changed my life."

She moaned as I squeezed her nipples through her thin shirt and bra, her ass pressing back against my dick. "What did you see?"

"I saw you. Here in this room. Over on that bed."

I watched in the mirror as her face went from full of pleasure to full of confusion. "What... what do you mean?"

I turned her around to face me, knowing this next tidbit was likely to embarrass her no matter how turned on she was. I quickly pushed her pants off her, groaning at the sight of her light pink thong. She didn't fight me, even when I unexpectedly lifted her up and placed her down on the top of the dresser. This made her the perfect height for me to bend down a little and get my mouth right at the same level as her already wet pussy.

I slowly pulled her panties to the side, a growl leaving me at the sight of her glistening lips. She canted her hips towards me, and I ran a finger gently up and down the skin I was about to put my mouth on. Meeting her eyes, I made the last of my confession.

"I saw you on your bed, touching that wet pussy of yours. You were topless, and I couldn't tear my eyes away from the way your pretty tits trembled with every thrust and rub of your fingers."

Her eyes had gone wide, her body stiffening in shock at my words. That's when I closed the distance and began eating her cunt like it was the only way for me to survive.

"Fuck, Liam, that's so embarrassing. I can't believe you saw that!" She struggled to get the words out between moans and sighs with every lick and nibble I took of her.

"I think I might've been able to forget the sight someday. I might have stayed... If I hadn't heard you moan my name right as you came." I'd pulled my mouth away from her to say the last words, sliding two fingers inside her tight, virgin hole before I dropped the last bomb on her. I dove back in, focusing my lips and tongue on her clit as I curled my fingers against the front wall of her pussy and rubbed, feeling the way she gushed around my fingers.

"You... heard... that?"

I pulled away one more time to meet her eyes when I answered her, never stopping the movements of my fingers inside her while I moved my thumb to her clit to rub the sensitive button in sync. "Yes. I watched my stepsister finger herself to thoughts of me, calling my name while she came. And even though I hadn't really seen her until that night, I knew it was the beginning of the end for me. I lay in bed for hours, Celeste, battling the desire I felt. Trying to forget the way you looked, how you sounded. After stroking myself to the memories and still not being able to let it go, I went out and got so fucking drunk so I wouldn't be able to remember anything."

"Oh my god," she cried out.

"But you want to know the worst part?" I asked, moving my thumb faster as her hips started to move up and down, fucking herself on my fingers and nearly making me come in my pants right there.

"What?" A word spoken on a gasp.

"I've never gotten over wanting to see my stepsister come again. No matter how wrong it is, it's the thought that pops into my head every time right before I come when I'm stroking my hard cock. And now that I've felt you, tasted you, seen you up close, I'm not sure I'll ever be able to think of anything ever again."

I felt her tighten around my fingers, and I pressed my lips against hers as she screamed her orgasm into my mouth, fingernails digging into my shoulders as she quivered, coming on her dresser and making me wonder just what it'd feel like to have her coming around my cock.

I rubbed her until I could tell she was getting too sensitive before slowly pulling my fingers out and licking them clean. She watched me with hazy eyes, and my cock throbbed hard at the taste of her on my tongue. I moved her panties back in place to cover her and gave her a light slap on the wet crotch that made her jolt. I gave her a wicked grin before helping her down, watching as she found a new pair of pants to put on before resuming packing.

I wasn't expecting her to act like nothing had happened, but I figured she needed a little time to process what had just happened.

"Can you get some stuff from downstairs for me?" Her voice was raspy, but I followed her lead with moving on for the moment.

"Yeah, just tell me what you need." I paid partial attention to her as she listed off the items, the other half of my brain wondering when exactly it was I'd fallen for her. It was something I'd realized while helping her figure out everything here. I'd gone from mild obsession to what I was pretty sure was love, and I was taking this flooding of her house as a sign to get on that and make her fall in love with me, too, before I lost what was probably the best thing to ever happen to me.

Chapter 18

Celeste

This was simultaneously the worst and best Friday I'd ever had. I was currently snuggled up in my warm, *dry* bed at Liam's place, the clock nearing midnight as I glanced at my phone. My body still tingled from the orgasm Liam had given me earlier, and my mind was still boggled at his confession.

Sixteen-year-old Celeste was so fucking embarrassed.

Twenty-seven-year-old Celeste was absolutely turned on. I groaned in frustration as I rolled to my back in the bed, my pussy pulsing again at the thought of Liam masturbating to me saying his name. Why was something so forbidden, so filthy, so goddamn hot?

My phone began to ring, and with everything that my mind had gone through today it didn't occur to me to think about who could possibly be calling me at midnight.

"Hello?"

There was a pause on the other end. "Cassie?"

I nearly corrected the man on the other line when my

brain finally caught up. *Fuck.* I pulled the phone away from my ear and saw I'd received the call through the phone sex app, and Alex was on the other end, and I should be answering as Cassie.

I hurried to put on a pleasant voice. "Oh, hi, Alex."

His dark chuckle sounded strained, but before I could get any words out, he spoke again. "I hope you don't mind me calling you without checking first, but I'm so fucking horny right now and I need you."

I purred into the phone, my body melting at the words. Even if he didn't know who I was, I knew I was talking to Liam. A small part of me was bothered that he'd call a woman he never met, when I, Celeste, was there and willing, but I shoved that thought aside.

"I'm actually very glad you called, because I'm already wet."

Liam's groan was loud, and I could've sworn I heard him in echo, once on the line and once through the walls of his house. I panicked a tiny bit, wondering if he'd be able to hear me as well and figure out who Cassie really was. I decided I would just keep it a little quieter right now. At least I knew Liam would be too busy to notice random sounds coming from my room.

"Oh, do you like that, Alex? Do you like knowing I'm in bed and touching myself under my panties, thinking of you and wishing you were here to touch me?"

"Fuck yes I do. I can just imagine how fucking good you'd look. Taste. How you're going to sound when you come with me over the phone."

It was my turn to moan, my fingers moving down into my panties like I'd said, rubbing my clit and sending me right to the edge in a second.

"Alex, I'm not going to last long tonight."

"Don't worry about that, baby, you can come as fast as you need to. As many times as you need to."

I let out a soft cry at his words, the roughness of his voice doing me in. I was already a mess, and I trembled under my fingers that I couldn't stop from sliding down further and playing in my wetness.

"I can hear how wet you are," I heard him groan into my ear. "Can you imagine what it would feel like coating my cock? If I were pumping in and out of that fucking tight pussy until your juices ran down my balls, soaking both of us? How hard I'd come inside you when you squeezed my dick while you came around it?"

"Yes, oh god, yes, I can." I pushed two fingers into my pussy, wishing they were Liam's fingers sliding inside instead. He knew all the right spots to hit in me, and even just two of his fingers stretched me out in a way that made me think of what it would feel like to have his cock stretching me out the same way.

"Are you going to come for me again, my filthy girl? You know I need to hear it. I'm squeezing my cock so hard right now, wishing it was you around me instead. Let me hear you, Cassie."

My legs shook as I cried out his name, my mind nothing but bliss as I came even harder this time than the first. His grunts filled my ear, dragging out my orgasm until my body sunk into the bed, hand still in my panties but just resting on my pubic bone now.

"Jesus, that was incredible, Celeste."

I hummed in agreement, then froze, my body going cold. "What... did you just say?"

"I said that was incredible, Celeste."

I shot up in bed, relaxed no longer. I couldn't even form any words, my brain short-circuiting.

"How the hell did you figure it out?"

"You think I haven't memorized the sound of your voice? The way you sound when you moan or sigh when you come? Do you really think I'd keep talking to some stranger when I had you? My heart knew you were Cassie long before my brain realized it. How did you know who I was? After all, you did call out my name a minute ago. My real name."

I thought back to my last orgasm, flushing when I realized I'd done exactly that. I was the first one to let the cat out of the bag, and I hadn't even realized it. That was what Liam did to me. Scrambled my brains until I was fucking everything up.

"God, this is the fucking longest day of my life," I groaned out as I fell back against the bed, my hand covering my eyes even though he wasn't even in my room to see me. "Can we pretend this never happened?"

"I doubt it. Now, tell me, Celeste. How did you figure it out?"

"Something you said to me the night of the benefit. After our dance."

"Ahh. So that's why you ran away that night. And pulled away later."

"Not that it helped," I grumbled out.

"And thank God for that." I scoffed, but he continued. "I'm serious. I, well, I really like you, Celeste. A lot. I hope you are comfortable here. And if you really need me to, we can pretend Alex and Cassandra never existed in our world."

"I would appreciate that." I was confused at the pang that filled my chest at my answer, but it was too much to deal with right now. "I like you a lot, too, Liam. Goodnight."

I hung up before either of us could keep talking, and I spent a sleepless night wondering what the hell I was going to do. I was sure I was already half in love with him, but how did he feel? Obviously, he wanted me. But I needed more than that.

I wasn't a virgin at twenty-seven because I was afraid of

sex or waiting for marriage. I was waiting for the right man, and the right time. For someone to make me want to rip my clothes off so he'd get inside me, and then cuddle with until we fell asleep. Equal parts dirty and cute.

That's what Liam gives you, my mind pointed out helpfully. I sighed, acknowledging how right that was. I was hopelessly gone for him, despite everything that was wrong about falling in love with my stepbrother.

"Oh my god, Liam, don't tell me you bought me more stuff!" I looked hopelessly over at my temporary roommate, distress and delight filling me all at the same time. I'd been here for a week now, and the torture of being so close to him and yet so far away was slowly driving me mad. Not to mention all the little gifts he'd been buying me, surprising me with when I got home from work. I don't know how he was managing it, but every day there'd been something. They were ridiculous, silly gifts that made me laugh. A pair of arm floaties, a life vest, and a mini canoe with accompanying paddles were among the treasures, all something to make me laugh about my house flooding. He somehow knew I needed that, and I was grateful for it.

This particular gift, however, was larger than the others. I had no idea what he could've gotten me this time, and I began to unwrap it cautiously.

"Just open it already, geez," he teased before helping me rip off a strip. My eyes widened, and I looked up at him as excitement filled me.

"You fucking didn't," I said. He only chuckled as I ripped apart the last of the wrapping, staring down at the gift he'd given me. My hands were full of a stack of premium painting canvases, high-quality paints – both acrylic and oil –, and brand-new brushes. Not to mention sketching pencils and a pad to go with. The enormity of what he'd given me hit me, and I hastily blinked back tears as I tried to swallow my emotions.

"Are those okay? I did a bunch of research, and the lady at the store assured me these were top quality. If you don't like them, we can take them back and exchange them." His nervous words made me look up at him, a weird laugh-sob leaving me before I set the stuff down on the table and launched into his arms. He caught me effortlessly, his arms a band of safety around my body as I clung to him in a grateful hug.

"You didn't have to do this for me, but thank you. Thank you so much." The words were barely a whisper, but when he squeezed me tighter and kissed my shoulder lightly, I knew he heard them.

"All I've been able to see since yesterday is how heart-broken you looked when we stopped at your house to get your art stuff."

He spoke in a gruff voice, and the devastation I felt yesterday when I'd realized at least half of my art supplies were ruined by the flood came back to hit me. I'd spent so much time, money, effort, blood sweat and tears for my supplies and into my paintings that it was like a piece of my heart was ripped out to see them ruined.

That Liam had not only noticed but researched and asked and bought new stuff for me meant more than he'd ever know. I'd put aside all my art dreams when my dad got sick and hadn't gotten a chance to pick it back up since, but with Liam's help and silent encouragement to keep going I knew it was time.

I also knew, with certainty, I was in love with him. Completely, totally gone for this man. Whatever reservations I'd had before were slowly whittling away in this last week with

Liam, and now they were nothing but dust. He had my heart, but there was one last thing I wanted to give him.

With that decision, I pulled myself from the circle of Liam's arms, gazing up at him with all the love I couldn't form words for. He looked down at me and I could swear I saw the same damn thing in his eyes.

We stood there for who knows how long before the doorbell chimed, breaking us out of our reverie.

"Ah, that must be the food I ordered," Liam said.

I sighed in mild frustration. "Liam, I said I would cook. You've ordered dinner at least three times this week, and I'm starting to feel useless."

"Well, then why don't you go pick a movie for once." He walked off towards the door like what he'd said wasn't completely ridiculous.

"What! You never let me pick the movie!"

He had the audacity to laugh, but before I could do or say anything about it, he opened the door. I shut my mouth, fuming as he talked to the delivery guy.

"Oh, why don't you pick a movie, since you never do," I mocked in a low voice while I stomped to the den and started browsing the DVD's. "Sure, Celeste, you can come cook in exchange for me giving you a freakin' home to stay in, except for the fact I order food all the damn time!"

A low chuckle sounded behind me and I whipped around to see him with arms full of delicious smelling food, watching me as I made fun of him.

"I don't sound like that."

"Oh yes you do! All high-handed and acting like you're not bossing me around when you are!"

I stood with my hands on my hips, glaring at him. He set the food down on the couch and came near me. I held out a hand to stop him from coming near since that usually scrambled my thoughts, but he merely took that hand and used it to pull me closer.

"Then why do you listen to me? I know you're stubborn enough to fight it. Is it because you like me bossing you around?"

"Absolutely not!" I protested loudly. Even a little too loudly to my own ears. A smug grin tilted his mouth and I wanted to smack it off and then kiss him.

"You keep lying to yourself, babe. Now," he said and let me go, "let's eat. What movie did you pick?"

I spun around and grabbed a random movie, trying to get his taunting words out of my head. *Did I like it?* He was right, I usually put up way more of a fight than this.

I mindlessly put the DVD in the player and went to sit on the opposite side of the couch from Liam, who managed to stay silent about it but couldn't help smiling. I grabbed the remotes and turned the TV on, then skipped through the previews to the menu.

"Ah, *"Mr. and Mrs. Smith"*. Good choice," Liam said as he handed over a carton of food. I opened it and my mouth watered at the sight of the smothered burrito. At least he ordered good food when he wouldn't let me cook.

"Thanks," I mumbled reluctantly. "And for the food."

"You're very welcome, Celeste."

We ate in silence, and when we both finished, Liam pulled me into his side so we could snuggle as had become our habit over the last few days. I wanted to protest since I was still slightly annoyed with him, but I couldn't help melting into him. His warmth and comfort called to me, and even though I was giving in, I wasn't really losing. After all, I got a pretty good deal too.

Everything was perfectly normal until we got to *that scene*. Where Brad Pitt and Angelina Jolie throw each other around while making out and grinding and shit. I'd never been particularly affected by it, but watching it now all tangled up with Liam had me imagining the two of us doing that exact same thing. My nipples hardened under my tank top, and I squirmed a little.

"You okay?" Liam's words were quiet, like he didn't want to interrupt the movie.

"I'm good." Was that my voice? It sounded all raspy, and I was sure Liam had noticed. He hummed in acknowledgement of my answer, but he shifted in his seat as well. At the same time, his hand that had been resting on my waist had relocated to right under my boob, his thumb now grazing the bottom swell every few seconds.

The light touch shouldn't have had me closing my eyes. It shouldn't have had my clit pulsing in my wet panties. But it did, and it made me wish he would move his damn hand higher already. I wasn't even paying attention to the movie anymore, my focus solely on that wicked thumb of his.

I shifted again in my seat, sighing his name aloud when that move put my tit right into the palm of his hand, the following gentle squeeze probably an automatic reaction from him.

"What are you doing to me, Celeste?"

Liam's question had me turning, shifting to my knees and climbing over him to straddle his lap. I felt his hardness under me and although it pressed into my pussy right where I needed it, I was more affected seeing the look of wonder on his face. I moved my hips over him, not trying to get either of us off but wanting to feel the friction.

"I want you to take my virginity."

I said the words before I could think about it. The moment felt right; I wanted him, he wanted me. I loved him, and I had a feeling he felt the same way even though neither of us had come out and said it.

I felt his cock jump underneath me and his hands tighten

on my hips at my words, and I knew he liked the idea. His words surprised me, however.

"No." I stopped moving, embarrassment automatically flooding me. Before I could move off his lap, Liam pulled me into him and placed a soft kiss on my lips. "What I meant is I'm not doing it tonight. I want it to be right for you. You deserve a special first time, and I want to give it to you."

Aww. I melted at his words, even as my pussy protested. "I don't really need all that. I'd be perfectly fine with pushing aside my shorts and panties and mounting you right here."

"Fuck, don't say that. I'm on a thin wire as it is." His hips thrust up into me, and I gasped, head going back. "I'm not fucking you tonight, but I will make you come. Do you think you can do it like this?"

"Yes, just please don't stop."

He didn't, not until I'd come with his hands guiding my hips, lips and tongue teasing my nipples through my tank top as we dry humped like teenagers.

After which we finished the movie and then went to our separate bedrooms where I'm sure he stroked himself to thoughts of me just like I was touching myself to thoughts of him, my heart beating hard in my chest just knowing that soon, he would have all of me.

Chapter 19

Liam

"Please come with me, I swear they won't mind." Celeste's voice was pleading, and I was already about to give in when she struck the final blow. "I need you there with me."

"All right, fine. What are the details?" I said the words with a smile, her pleased sounds at my acquiescence enough to calm my nervousness at the prospect of officially meeting her friends.

"Yay! Okay, so we're going to meet downtown at this cool new restaurant Anthony got us reservations for. Since Luke is leaving town for a job in a couple of weeks, we wanted to throw a going away party for him."

"And when is it?"

"Tomorrow night. And don't forget, I have that meeting with the insurance adjuster in the afternoon so I'll be home late."

"Right, you sure you don't want me to go with you to that?" I sat back at my desk, cradling my phone between my ear and my shoulder as I relaxed. Hearing her call our place home had that effect on me every time.

I was currently the last one at the office, needing to finish some things I hadn't gotten to the last couple of days since I'd been completely preoccupied with Celeste's confession.

I want you to take my virginity.

I started to harden in my pants again, just like I did every time I replayed the words, the way she'd looked when she'd said them.

"I'm sure, but thank you again for the offer." I could tell she was smiling, even over the phone. I heard some pans banging together in the background, and my stomach growled at the thought of her cooking. She'd proven to be an excellent chef during the couple of weeks she'd been with me, and I could tell she liked doing it.

"What are you making?"

"Bacon jalapeno mac and cheese bake."

My mouth watered, and I immediately began to shut everything down. "I'm on my way home."

She laughed, and the sound lit me up like it always did. "See you in a bit."

<hr />

"And *then* he was like, 'Well, miss, it looks like you're shit out of luck because we're only going to cover about fifty percent of the damages and losses'. I mean, obviously he didn't say it like that, but that was his tone!"

Celeste was incredibly adorable when she was frustrated. I would never tell her that, but it was all I could do not to smile as I watched her rant out of the corner of my eye, arms flailing all over the place as she spoke. We were on our way to meet up with her friends, and she was updating me on the meeting she'd had with the insurance agent at her place. Which apparently didn't go well.

"What a dick," I supplied helpfully when it seemed like she was waiting for a response.

"Yes! What a dick!" She sighed, head falling back against the passenger seat and rubbed her forehead. "I mean, fifty percent is better than nothing, but it's still going to cost a pretty good chunk of money to get my place habitable again."

I reached over and slipped my hand in hers. "Don't worry, babe. We'll figure it out."

"We?" She raised an eyebrow at me, and I nodded.

"Yes, we. You don't think I'd let you handle this alone, did you?"

"I dunno. I just figured it was my house, so it was my responsibility."

"Maybe, but you're not alone in this. Now, let's change the subject. Where the fuck am I going?"

The question brought forth the giggle I wanted to hear, and I squeezed her hand while she guided me to the parking lot. We walked in together still holding hands, and Celeste immediately spotted her friends. She dragged me behind her, waving and grinning as we made our way over. I started to get nervous all over again, wondering if I would pass this test. I had already met them, but I hadn't stayed long that night at the bar. I'd been too wound up with memories and needed to escape before I had said or done something completely stupid.

"Hey man, it's good to see you again." Anthony was the first to speak up, stretching across the table to clasp my hand in his.

"Likewise," I responded with a smile. I turned to Luke and we exchanged greetings, then Madison who surprised me by pulling me in for a hug.

"Thanks for taking care of my girl," she whispered quickly into my ear.

"It's nothing," I whispered back. "I'd do it for anyone."

She pulled back and gave me a look that said she didn't quite believe the little white lie. We all sat down, and immediately the three of them started asking Celeste questions about her house, offering help and advice. I could see the struggle she fought inside to accept the help. Obviously, her friends knew her well, because they didn't push her about anything, instead just offering up their services.

"Okay, that's enough about me! We're here for Luke, who has a very exciting opportunity!"

Everyone took the topic change in stride, and I figured now was a good time to jump into the conversation. "Celeste was saying you're going to be out of town for a few months for a work thing?"

"Yep," Luke said. "Four months to be exact. I'm going to help train some people in a new office we're expanding to."

"What is it you do?"

"I'm a senior app developer. Lots of technical stuff, but basically I help build and fix apps as well as discover and bring in new developers."

"So, what he's saying is under the pressed clothes and tanned skin, he's a giant nerd," Celeste added in a teasing voice.

Luke sniffed. "We prefer the term geek, thank you very much."

Anthony and Madison began to argue with him about whether there was even a difference between the two, and I could tell this wasn't a new discussion. I looked over at Celeste who was just shaking her head with a smile. She looked over at me, and I could see a tinge of sadness there that I couldn't place the reason behind.

"They have this argument every time he says that," she stage whispered.

"And I'm guessing you instigate it every time?"

"Yes!" The other three obviously heard my question amidst their own conversation, as they were the ones who responded before picking up where they left off. Celeste and I looked at each other and both started laughing.

By the time Celeste and I left, I felt like I'd been friends with them for years. They welcomed me without hesitation, and I'd never felt so accepted other than when Travis and I had become friends. I knew he'd fit right in with the group, and something about the rightness of blending my and Celeste's lives made me excited for the future.

"I had a great time, Celeste, thank you for making me come with you." I said the words to Celeste as I parked at my house and turned to see a devilish smirk on her lips. Those tempting, pouty lips. Her aqua eyes were a tad hazy from the drinks she'd had at dinner, but she seemed to be carrying herself well despite that.

"I know a few other ways to make you *come* with me," she purred.

I groaned, knowing I wouldn't be doing anything with her while she was this close to drunk. "None of that, minx. Let's get you inside and to bed."

"Hmm, inside. I like the sound of that."

"Damn it, Celeste, I'm not fucking you while you've been drinking."

"Party pooper," she grumbled, but thankfully relented for the moment. I got out and helped her inside, directing her towards the rooms upstairs.

"Can you get me a glass of water?" Her polite request was simple enough, and I watched her make her way up the stairs safely before heading to the kitchen.

I got the water and brought it to her, knocking on her partly open door before stepping inside. I froze in the doorway, taking in the glimpse of completely naked skin I caught before she slipped a large t-shirt over her body.

No bra. No panties. My mouth went dry, and I almost took a drink of the water I was holding.

"Oh, thank you. I hope you don't mind if I go paint." She took the glass and gulped it down quickly.

"Of course not." The words were a croak, so I cleared my throat before continuing, "You know you're welcome to use that room whenever you want."

I'd cleared out a room in the basement of my house that had a big window, which was perfect for ventilating any fumes that resulted from her work, and told her to go crazy. She had agreed on the condition I wouldn't go in there without permission, something I had readily agreed to. I was dying to peek, but I wanted her to know she could trust me.

"Okay. And I promise, even if I'm not sober now, this water and the smell of paint will clear my head more than enough."

"Sounds good." I swallowed hard, unable to stop myself from asking the next question. "Do you... Are you going to put underwear on?"

"Hmm? Oh, no, I usually paint naked. Makes me feel freer."

I cursed under my breath and started backing out of the room, already picturing her in nothing but swipes and splotches of paint.

"Okay. Have fun. Goodnight." I turned and bolted, pretending like I didn't hear her husky laugh trail me all the way to my shower where I took my frustration in my own hands.

Chapter 20

Liam

Celeste and I were both on the edge, teasing each other and coming so fucking close to taking that next step but holding back for some reason. Neither of us could pinpoint it, but I can say for myself that I got some kind of perverse pleasure from seeing how many times I could make her come with my mouth or my fingers or just rubbing against her before she passed out in my bed.

Where I'd made sure she'd slept every night since her last painting escapade. I might not be fucking her yet, but I was at least going to sleep with her in my arms.

She'd voiced a concern about our personal relationship affecting our work one, but I'd pointed out she technically worked for Travis so there was nothing wrong with it. It'd taken a little convincing, but after eating her to orgasm she agreed it wasn't a big deal.

The only time our relationship was an inconvenience at work was when we were in the same room together– like now, for example. Travis, Noelle, Celeste, and I were all in a meeting going over what needed to be finished for the next art showing we were scheduled to have in two days.

Since this one was set up for local artists to get their names and art out into the world, we were going over the last-minute details on how it was going to be set up. I was supposed to be listening, but all I could think about was pushing up Celeste's blue pencil skirt to see what panties she was wearing today—if any. I usually caught a glimpse before we left, but she'd somehow managed to get dressed while I was in the shower and I'd missed the show.

"What do you think, Liam?"

I jerked my eyes from Celeste to Travis. "Sounds good to me."

Smothered snorts of laughter followed my statement. I could feel my face heat, knowing I'd made it obvious I wasn't paying attention.

"You must've misheard me," Travis said with a knowing grin. "I was asking what you thought we should do with the two open exhibition spots we have. Should we see if artists who are already participating want two spots, or should we try to find more people in the next twenty-four hours?"

I tapped my fingers on the tabletop, glancing at Celeste who seemed to be taking notes. I was pretty sure she had enough pieces to show, so why wasn't she saying anything?

"I have one person in mind, but I would try asking, uh, Leona?"

"Leonora Scadero? Paints hyper-realism?" Noelle shuffled through papers, finding the one she needed and holding it up. I snapped my fingers in agreement.

"Yep, that's the one."

"All right, I can take care of that," she said scribbling something down.

"And this mystery person? When can I expect an update on that?" Travis asked.

I turned back to Travis. "Give me until tomorrow morning. I'll have an answer by then, and we'll go from there for that open spot."

"Perfect. All right, unless anyone has something else, you're all free to go."

Everyone started picking their stuff up and leaving the room, and I quickly followed Celeste out.

"Celeste, can I borrow you for a sec?" She turned to me and gave me a smoldering look that had my cock twitching in my pants. *Not a good time,* I mentally scolded.

She readily followed me into my office, shutting the door and coming over to me where I'd sat in my chair. I didn't need to say anything to get her to straddle me; it's what we both wanted despite that not being the reason for me asking her in here. She leaned forward, wrapping her arms lightly around my neck, and placed a gentle kiss on my lips. We stayed there for a moment, and then she pulled back.

"I already know what you're going to say, and although I appreciate the thought, the answer is no."

"No, you don't want to show off your talent?"

"You haven't even seen my paintings or sketches; how do you know I have talent?"

"Because I know you. You don't do anything half-assed. You wouldn't have gone to school for art if it wasn't something you're good at, but more than that, you wouldn't have gone if it wasn't something you were passionate about."

"While all of that is true, even if I was merely good at art, it doesn't mean I deserve to hang my works up next to people who do."

She slid off my lap and straightened her clothes, walking away like the conversation was over. Jumping up from my chair, I reached out for her and stopped her.

"Hang on a sec, Celeste, I'm not done. I really think you should do this."

She shook my hand off with more force than I expected, and I pulled my hand back, shocked.

"Don't tell me what to do, Liam. If I wanted other people to see them, I would've taken care of it. My paintings are none of your business, so just leave it alone."

"Everything about you is my business." My words were forceful and stern, the heat of frustration and hurt from her rejection of me from that part of her life. The color was high on her cheeks and her once kind, aqua eyes had narrowed and turned to stone.

"What makes you think that? Because you're my *stepbrother*? Because you've made me come?" She scoffed. "We're not together. We're not even fucking, Liam. You don't have the right."

Each word sliced through my heart, and before I could respond she yanked the door open and stormed out, slamming it shut behind her.

"Fuck!" That was not how I expected that conversation to go at all. I ran my hand roughly through my hair and sat back down in my chair with a groan. Something inside my chest ached and I rubbed the spot with my palm as I contemplated everything.

The one thing I knew for certain was I needed to apologize for pushing her too far– even if I thought her response had been unnecessarily cruel. Maybe we weren't fucking, and yeah, maybe we'd never come out and officially stated what we were, but I felt like we were close enough for her to trust me.

I figured I might as well go apologize now, so I left my office in search of her. After combing the building and not finding even a hint of her, I headed to Travis' office.

"Come on in," Travis called out after my short knock. He took one look at my face and knew why I was there. "She went home early. Said she was feeling 'sick'. And before you head there to check on her, I would suggest giving her some time to 'feel better' first."

He didn't directly throw his fingers up into the air to quote his words, but the implication was there. He must've seen how angry she was, and when I'd come calling shortly after, he'd figured out it was my fault. I sighed heavily and gave a short thank you to him before heading back to my office and using my work to keep my mind busy.

I returned home after taking care of everything I possibly could at work, and I opened the door with a bit of guilt, knowing it was late and Celeste would know I'd avoided coming home because of our argument. She'd probably think it was because I was angry with her, but really it was because I didn't know how to fix things between us.

I stepped in the house and called her name, pausing to listen for an answer, I heard nothing, so I went up to my room to see if she was already asleep. Nothing in there had changed since this morning, so that was a bust. I loosened my tie and chucked it across the room, knowing where I needed to go.

A few moments later I was knocking on the door to the room I'd given to Celeste for her painting, noticing the light shining underneath the door. After getting no response, I knocked louder, opening the door a tad to call to her.

"Celeste?"

When I still heard nothing, I began to feel slightly concerned. I wanted to make sure she hadn't passed out or hurt herself, but I knew she'd specifically asked me not to go in without her invitation. I hesitated for a minute, but decided that her safety was more important than her pride.

I quickly opened the door and looked around. No Celeste, but what I did see had me momentarily forgetting my search, making my breath stutter in my chest. In the middle of the room facing the door was a canvas propped up on an easel.

The painting was half-done, but I could already see it was going to be outstanding.

And not just because the subject was someone I was more than familiar with.

My own tense jaw filled up the bottom of the canvas, the paint trailing up my face and filling in the details of my facial scruff and cheekbone. My one finished eye was a swirl of black and grays, intensity and passion obvious as my own stare bored into me.

Was this how she saw me?

I shook myself out of my stupor, closing my jaw as my original reason for coming in here came back to me. If Celeste wasn't in my room or her painting room, where the hell was she? Panic filled me, and I moved away from the door, searching each room as I came across it. I called out her name as I rushed around, pounding up the stairs as I became more frantic.

Just as I reached the landing, a door down the hallway opened and Celeste walked out, rubbing her eyes.

"Liam? What's the matter?"

I stalked towards her, wrapping her in my arms and kissing the hell out of her, my relief at seeing her still here overwhelming. She froze for a moment but in the next second started to return the kiss, wrapping her arms around me and diving in.

I tore my mouth away from hers and we stared at each other, breathing heavily. Her eyes were at half-mast, a mix of sleepiness and desire.

"I'm sorry," I said into the silence. She blinked a few times and I paused to give her mind a chance to catch up. "I shouldn't have pushed you like I did. I didn't mean to upset you."

She sighed. "I apologize too. I... wasn't very nice. I didn't mean to make you feel like you weren't important to me."

Her words soothed the hurt from before, and I wrapped her in my arms again for a tight hug.

"We're even then, I suppose. Except why the hell are you in your old room?"

Even in the semi-dark, I could see the blush on her cheeks as she avoided my gaze.

"Well, you didn't come home when you normally do, and I was upset enough that I figured we could both use some room to cool down."

I tilted her head up to look at me, so she could see how serious I was. "I'll never be mad enough at you to shut you out like that. Never. But, if you ever 'run' from me again as you did today, I won't hesitate to light a fire on your naughty little bottom."

I turned her towards *our* room. "Get in bed, I'll be in in a minute." Slapping her ass, I watched her giggle and hustle off to our bed.

I went back down to the office with her paintings, intending to merely turn off the light and shut the room up. My finger was on the switch, but my curiosity got the better of me. I glanced up through the ceiling, guilt swirling through me like Celeste could see what I was about to do.

I could feel my heartbeat speed up as I stepped into the room and walked towards the wall that had canvases facing backwards. I turned the one closest to me around and stared. And stared. Turning it back, I moved to the next one, doing the same thing. I moved down the wall, looking at every single finished painting.

Blowing out what breath was left in my body, I faced the last canvas back to the wall like it'd been before. I moved out of the room and turned the light off, shutting the door like nothing had changed.

I went up the stairs and to my room, undressing and

climbing in behind the already asleep Celeste. She hummed with content, turning into my arms and snuggling in.

I stayed awake for another hour or two, working through a plan.

I was going to do something really fucking stupid. It was also a great idea, but I knew it was a risk. I knew it might cost me the only person I'd ever fallen in love with, but I also knew it would be worth it. Celeste was worth it, and it was about damn time she knew it.

Chapter 21

Celeste

After my and Liam's simple midnight apologies and his warning for my 'naughty butt' – would he really spank me and why did the thought turn me on? – I was feeling much better. I knew he'd only been trying to encourage me, but the thought of displaying my art for everyone to see freaked me the hell out. I put my heart and soul into those things, and I just wasn't ready for everyone to see inside me like that. The art world could be cruel, and I didn't think I could handle the rejection.

Unfortunately, I made the mistake of telling Madison about what happened, and now she was telling me the exact same thing Liam had.

"Seriously, Celeste, I've seen some of your stuff. Other than your dad, I'm pretty sure I'm the only one who has. Have you even shown them to Liam?"

I shook my head, and then remembered that we were on the phone so she couldn't see me.

"No, I haven't."

A screech sounded, and I jerked in pain as it blasted my eardrum through my Bluetooth earpiece. I was in the store-room at work sorting through the art for the show tomorrow.

"Celeste! You have to let people see your art. See *you* if you want to be successful in this world. And don't tell me that's not what you want, you've been talking about it for years. Well, at least until your dad got sick. You might have shelved that dream to take care of him and all the bills that followed, but it doesn't need to keep collecting dust."

"First of all, never scream into the phone like that again, you nearly broke my ear ball."

"Ear ball is not a thing," she interrupted.

"Yes, it is. And second, I barely have any real training or experience. My art is just... me."

"Celeste," Madison said in a sympathetic voice, "that's exactly what art *is*. It's pieces of the artist laid out for everyone to see. It's personal, it's passion, it's heartache and love and a myriad of other things. Training is not necessary. You know that! Some of your favorite artists are self-taught. So why should you be different?"

I stopped what I was doing, taking in her words. She was right, but it didn't make me feel any more comfortable with the idea. Someday I'd get my stuff out there, but I just didn't feel ready for that step yet. I knew she'd badger me about this until I gave in, so I changed the subject.

"So how about those Red Sox?"

I grinned at Madison's laughter. "Smooth, Celeste. You don't even pay attention to baseball."

"Maybe it's something new I'm a fan of."

"If that were true, you'd know that the Red Sox season is over already."

"Damn," I whispered.

"But if you want to change the subject, we could talk about how it's going with Liam."

"Or we could definitely not."

"Ooh, that bad huh?"

"Actually, it's not too bad. We're progressing even if a bit slowly for my taste, but we're getting along well."

"What are you going to do now that your house is almost habitable?"

The one thing I'd been trying to avoid thinking about. In fact, the house was supposed to be ready to go back to today. I just didn't want to go back. Back to a quiet house and lonely bed. Even going back to my separate room at Liam's house last night had been so hard for me to do, and that was when I was angry. What was it going to feel like when I was in a completely different house?

"I don't think I'm going to tell him yet. I will eventually, but I want a little more time with him." We both fell quiet, and that's when I realized something. "Hey! I thought I said I didn't want to talk about Liam. Bitch."

"Well then I guess you better come up with a better topic, or I'll keep bugging you about it."

"In that case, I guess it's only fair for me to check in on how you and Luke are doing."

"Well, since he's away for the next few months, we've decided to use it as an opportunity to bond in a different way. Kind of treating it like a long-distance thing, using Skype and the phone to get to know each other again."

"Oh, that's a good idea. Is it hard?"

"I... don't know. We've been a little distant anyway, so it's kind of awkward. We've known each other for years, for as long as I can remember. But we both feel so different, it's like I don't actually know him at all."

"I can't imagine what that's like."

"I wish I never knew."

The sadness in her voice was palpable. I hurt for my best

143

friend, but there was nothing I could do to help. "Well I hope it helps, this plan of yours."

"Me too." Quiet fell between us once again, but only for a few seconds. When Madison spoke again, it was with a fake, bright voice. "Now, tell me, what are you wearing to the event?"

I went into detail about the outfit I'd gotten yesterday after leaving work early, but my thoughts lingered on her words about my paintings. Was it a mistake to say no? Was I a coward for not wanting anyone to see?

After saying farewell to Madison, I hurried to gather all the remaining pieces for the exhibit and carted them to the hall where we'd be displaying them. When I got there Travis was already moving stuff around, so I jumped right in. We worked in silence, only speaking when I had a small question and he had an answer. Everything was labeled so it was easy to do.

"Did Leonora have some more stuff ready then?" I saw a couple of empty spots saved with her name on sticky notes when Travis and I had set everything up.

"She did, and seemed very excited to contribute some more."

The comment hit me square in the chest and I glanced over at Travis, wondering if Liam had told him about me. His face was clear, and I didn't see anything in his gaze to suggest he knew, so I relaxed. I looked over at another wall that was bare, leaving room for several large paintings.

"What's going over there?"

"Liam was able to get someone to contribute their art. I don't know who," he said before I could ask. "He said they wished to remain anonymous. So we are honoring that I suppose. He said they were exceptional pieces, and that it would be worth it to show them."

Hmm. "All right then. So that's it for today?"

"Yep. You are free to go. See you in the morning for the final touches!"

"Have a good night, Travis!"

I left the office, excited to get home and start dinner. I loved watching Liam enjoy the food I cooked. Even if I made something simple, he ate it voraciously and looked at me like I was a miracle. I could imagine any woman would do whatever they could to get that kind of look from someone as gorgeous as Liam.

That, and he usually thanked me with an orgasm or two afterwards. I grinned wickedly to myself at that thought, my body already beginning to throb with excitement. I wasn't going to think about the fact my house was probably done and I'd been unable to think of a realistic reason to stay with Liam anymore. Instead, I was going to steal as much extra time with him as possible.

Chapter 22

Liam

I followed the sound of Travis and Celeste talking, finding them looking around the event room with happy, excited faces. I looked around, hands in my pockets to hide my shaking hands. All the art was up on the walls, save for the unknown artist's work. I gulped, thinking of the secret I was holding back from the two people in front of me who finally noticed I was there.

"Oh, Liam! There you are. We've finished everything up here, so Travis was just about to let me go."

"Yeah, great timing there. You missed all the work."

He and Celeste laughed, and I chuckled nervously. "Sorry, I had to go pick up the paintings for the open space there."

"Perfect! I can help get them set up," Celeste said and started walking my way.

"No!" My vehemence startled them both, and I cleared my throat, hoping the sweat beading on my forehead wasn't obvious. "Sorry, what I meant was no, I have something else for you to do. Travis can handle them himself. Right?"

I turned to Travis, who was looking at me oddly, but agreed. "Yeah, I've got this. In the back of your car then?"

"Yeah. I'll leave it here for you, and we can take her car." I gestured at the two of us, and Travis nodded in agreement for the plan. "I labeled each canvas with the order to hang them in, although I'm sure you could have figured it out."

"Thanks," Travis said sarcastically with an eye roll.

I placed a hand on Celeste's back and guided her out of there, ignoring her protests about being able to help.

"Trust me, babe, what I've got planned is much more exciting."

After all, I needed to keep her distracted long enough to not even think about going into her painting room at the house before she had to get ready for the event. I needed to make sure she didn't notice the missing canvasses, the ones I'd loaded carefully into my car after she'd left this morning, and Travis was about to hang on the empty wall in the room we'd just left.

I knotted my tie for the third time, my nerves having got the best of me and making it more than difficult to make it look like an adult was tying it and not a child. My hands were moist and shaking, second-guessing myself for what I had done.

I could hear Celeste humming in the bathroom as she put the finishing touches on herself, perfectly content. I had a feeling that was going to change once she'd seen for her own eyes the evidence of my sneakiness.

"I'm ready if you are," Celeste said and stepped out of the bathroom. The silver dress she wore hugged her curves, the folds of the fabric drawing the eyes all along her body. When she moved, an aqua sheen that matched her eyes shimmered iridescently, and I couldn't help the way my jaw dropped and my cock hardened to full mast in mere seconds. Her curled hair caressed the bare skin of her shoulders and back, practically begging for me to wrap it in my hands and hold her still while I ravaged her.

She came over to me and brushed away the hands grabbing the fabric of my tie, doing it for me while wearing a satisfied smile. I let her, breathing in her scent and relishing these moments before everything blew up.

Thirty minutes later we were back at the office, about to walk through the doors when I pulled her to me and planted a kiss on her. I'd surprised her, and she didn't get the chance to respond in kind before I pulled away.

"You know I care about you, right?"

"Yes..." Her forehead scrunched, confusion obvious in the drawn-out word.

I took a deep breath, then nodded. "All right, let's go in."

I opened the door and ushered her in, guiding her to the doors of the event hall where she stepped through and looked around at all the people milling about, conversations being held in quiet murmurs and exclamations as they studied the art.

I knew the moment she saw what I had done, her steps freezing and her body going ramrod straight.

"You did this, didn't you, Liam?" I flinched at the utter coldness of the words. "How could you?"

I didn't answer, looking over her head to see the paintings I'd stolen from her room at the house. There were six in total, and I was taken away by them for the second time.

Her paintings had gathered a small crowd, people too stunned to move on for minutes as they looked them over.

It was a series of people, although you couldn't really tell at first glance. It wasn't until you took a second or third glance to see the figures in the swirl of colors.

The first two had images of two nude people, a man and a woman, reaching out to each other from the separate canvasses, a mix of cool blues, greens, and purples.

The second set had the same two people finally touching, the spot where their hands gripped each other's forearms now a wild burst of warm reds, yellows, and oranges. Both the man and woman's groin areas held hints of the warm colors, like each other's touch had begun to warm them. The woman's breasts and the man's chest also bore the hints, like their hearts had finally begun to beat inside them.

The third and final set of canvasses depicted them twined around each other, a sensual and comforting embrace that blasted the last of reserves from their bodies, the two figures now full of fire and heat.

In all, the paintings told the story of two lovers who brought out the fire and passion in each other, that while they had been searching and looking for the other, they had grown cold and wanting. It evoked a restlessness you felt while you were away from the person you loved. It made you want to find someone who you could make burn bright in life and did the same for you.

It showed the painter's desire for that kind of connection, the hope and fear and longing and all-consuming need for that one person. It stripped you bare.

I was stripped bare now, moving around to face Celeste and deal with the consequences.

"I'm not going to ask for your forgiveness, because I know I don't deserve it. I know I've broken your trust by ignoring your wishes, invading your space, and even your privacy. I just ask you to take a moment and *see*. Look at the people, their faces as they gaze at what you've done. No one knows your name, or that it was you. You don't have to admit anything, but you need to see you are worthy of being up on these walls, you deserve to be adored for everything you are and what you've done. What you can do."

I held my breath after my speech, waiting to see what she said. She stared at me, her eyes dark with betrayal and hurt. I could also see fear, probably at the thought no one would like what she'd created.

"I need a fucking drink."

With that, she turned away from me and went to the open bar, ordering something and gulping it down in one go before motioning for another. Concern filled me, but I knew she needed space from me so she could take it in.

"Whoever this unknown artist is, I have to commend you for getting these paintings. They are... indescribable. I'm tempted to buy them for myself."

I looked over to Travis, nodding in agreement. "I know the feeling."

"And you're not gonna tell me who it is?"

"It's not my place."

He hummed, taking a drink of what was probably scotch in his glass. "Well, everyone seems to love them. Not to mention all the other paintings we've got. I think we're going to do well tonight, my friend."

He clapped me on the shoulder and walked away to mingle with others.

I felt triumphant; I knew people would love Celeste's paintings. I watched the woman in question grab a third drink from the bar before walking off. She walked around the room, chatting with people about the artwork and completely avoiding her own. I kept my eyes on her the entire time, making sure she stayed safe and coherent.

Finally, she realized she'd been to every other section besides her own. I watched as she seemed to steel herself, walking forward on shaky legs. I followed behind her, keeping a safe distance but wanting to see what happened. As she approached, someone standing there turned and asked her a question.

"I'm not sure," I heard Celeste say as I got close. "They asked to remain anonymous."

"Well, I would like to pass on my congratulations to them. These pieces are remarkable."

Surprise ran through Celeste, stiffening her up. "You... really think so?"

"Absolutely. Can you not see what the artist was feeling when they painted them? Every brushstroke, every color placement. It all holds a piece of their soul, which is the definition of art. Every time an artist creates something, they put a part of themselves into it. It should show emotion and evoke the same in the viewers."

"*The principles of true art is not to portray, but to evoke.*"

My quoting of Jerry Kosinski had both women turning to face me, Celeste with a small frown and the other with a bright smile.

"Yes, exactly. It's good to see you again, Liam."

"And you, Serena." We both came in for a casual hug, and as we parted I caught the wide-eyed look on Celeste's face.

"Serena, as in Serena Olivas?"

"That's me! And you are?" She held out her hand politely for Celeste to shake, and Celeste did so with stars in her eyes.

"I'm Celeste. Thompson. Oh my god, I'm sorry to freak out like this but I am a huge fan of yours."

Serena laughed lightly. "Oh, honey, no worries. Being famous in the art world gives me more privacy than other celebrities since it's mostly my name that's famous and not my face."

"Yeah, but you... I mean, you're an amazing artist. I've looked up to you for years. Your painting, *The Way We Are*, was the reason I got into painting in the first place."

"Ah yes," Serena said with a dreamy look in her eyes.

"That was one of my absolute favorites. Are you an artist as well, then?"

I watched their back and forth with fascination, willing Celeste to come clean about herself. I was disappointed when after a moment, she merely said, "Something like that."

Serena looked at her, and I saw a subtle shift in her face as she glanced from the paintings on the wall to Celeste and then back again. She had probably figured it out, but I knew she wouldn't say anything.

"Well, I suggest you keep with it. If it's something you love, then never let it go." With those parting words, she walked off to look at other pieces, leaving Celeste and me alone. I watched Celeste as she stared after Serena, then turned to me.

"Did that just fucking happen?"

I held back the laughter that wanted to burst from me, and instead responded in a voice quiet enough she would be the only one to hear. "You mean, did one of the most famous names in the art world tell you your paintings were remarkable? Then, yes."

Celeste's cheeks burned, and she lifted her glass to finish the last of her drink. "I need another drink."

This time, I let out the laughter I was holding in, letting her walk off so she could mull over what had happened.

Another hour and a half later, things were winding down at the gallery showing when Serena came up to me. She followed my gaze, landing on Celeste who was leaning against a wall for support, staring at her paintings with a contemplative look on her face.

"So, this mysterious artist."

"What about them?"

Serena waited until I was looking at her to continue. "Does she not understand what kind of talent she has?"

I blew out a breath. "Not a clue. At least, she didn't before. She might now."

"Good. I expect to see these paintings at my office next week."

I felt my eyebrows raise high, up to my hairline. "You bought them?"

"Absolutely I did. I fell in love with them the moment I walked in the door. You really think I'd let them go to someone else?"

We both chuckled at that. I'd met Serena while coming up in the business side of the art world, and we had become fast friends while bulldozing over everyone else.

Celeste pushed away from the wall too quickly, nearly falling over before catching herself and giggling into her hand. She stumbled her way across the room to the bar, leaving her glass there and sitting on a stool, head in her hands. I turned back to Serena.

"I've got something to take care of."

She grinned at me and winked. "I figured you would say that. Have a good night."

"You as well."

I went over to Celeste, sitting down next to her, I gave her a minute. She mumbled something to me, but I couldn't understand the words.

"What?"

She sighed, lifted her face from her hands, looking at me. "You can say it."

I raised an eyebrow at her in question.

"I mean you can say 'I told you so'. I deserve it."

"I don't want to say that. I wasn't intending to prove you wrong or prove myself right. I wanted you to know you can do what you love and make a name for yourself. That's all it was. I was just here to give you a shove in the right direction."

"I'm still pissed at you. You had no right to go behind my back."

"I can accept that." I thrummed my fingers on the counter. "Your paintings sold, you know."

She drew in a sharp breath, then choked on her own spit. When she got her breath back, she gripped my shoulders and leaned in.

"You're serious? Because if this is a joke, it's not fucking funny."

"I'm one hundred percent serious. I wouldn't lie about that."

"What is happening?"

I threw my head back and laughed. "Life, babe. Now, let's go home. You need to sleep those drinks off."

"Yeah, you're probably right." She slid off the stool and right into my waiting arms. I wrapped her up tight into my side, bearing most of her weight as I directed her out the doors. I got her buckled into the passenger seat of my car without too much trouble and started home.

I was pretty sure she'd fallen asleep since she was quiet, her breathing even while slumped in the seat. I was wrong, however. Her voice was surprisingly clear when she spoke up just a minute or two out from my place.

"Thank you for pushing me tonight. I'm not happy about the way you did it, but I'm not too stubborn to see where you were coming from." She turned to me and placed a hand on my thigh, squeezing. She shifted, and I couldn't help but notice the way the skirt of her dress had pushed up, dangerously close to exposing her panties.

I gulped and looked away, ignoring my dick coming to life in my pants. "You're welcome. I'm sorry for breaking my promise to you in order to do it."

"I want to do something for you."

"Oh? And what's that?"

In lieu of a verbal answer, she slid her hand across my

thigh and cupped the outline of my half-hard cock. I sucked in a breath and tightened my hands on the steering wheel, making the last turn into my driveway. Parking and shutting off the car, I turned to face Celeste.

"I want to make you come."

Chapter 23

Celeste

"I know you won't do anything to me after I've been drinking," I continued to say, "but will you let me do things to you?"

He raised a sardonic eyebrow. "My filthy virgin stepsister thinks she can make me come, does she? Even after drinking all night?"

My quickened breath sounded so loud in the enclosed space of Liam's car.

"Can I confess something?" The sultry words left me and seemed to put him in a trance as I unbuckled my belt and maneuvered around so I was on my knees, facing him.

"Of course," he breathed out.

"I've never sucked a cock before." My hand stroked along his length, the hardening bulge in his pants a direct target for my advances. "But I dream about what you taste like, what you'd feel like in my mouth."

"Jesus." He closed his eyes momentarily, then grabbed my

wrist to stop me from stroking him anymore. "We need to get inside. Now."

I didn't need to be told twice. I scrambled to get out, not caring that the dress I'd put on had ridden up my legs and exposed my ass to him. When I heard a low growl behind me, I knew he'd seen I'd decided to skip the panties tonight.

I took a deep breath of the cool night air once I made it out, then turned to find Liam coming towards me, color high on his cheeks. I licked my lips, an obvious move, but it had the effect I was looking for. In the next second, I was slung over his shoulder and clenching onto his waist as I giggled. He stormed into the house and up the stairs, flinging me onto the bed where I bounced twice before settling.

Liam already had his suit jacket and tie thrown across the room, staring at me with an intensity that had my heart beating hard and pussy dripping wet in a second while he unbuttoned his shirt.

"Wait," I exclaimed as he moved to take his shirt off. "I want you like that."

He raised an eyebrow again but did as I asked. I got to my knees on the bed, doing my best to steady myself as I stripped off the only article of clothing I had on.

"Good Lord," Liam said on a groan once I was bared to him. My nipples puckered hard as his eyes roamed over my full tits, and I let my arms hang at my sides so he could look his fill.

"You want to taste me, dirty girl?" His words made me shiver and I nodded vigorously. My head swam a bit from the effects of the alcohol, but it had mostly worn off by that point.

"I've been wanting it for weeks. You've never let me. You distract me from it by going down on me, and I want to return the favor."

I crawled towards him and slid off the edge of the bed right to my knees in a graceful move I never would've thought I was capable of sober, much less tipsy. Reaching out, I grabbed the fabric of his pants by his thighs and pulled him towards me. I started to undo his buckle, and I looked up at him with eyes wide.

"Don't you want to feel my lips around you? Don't you want to feel my tongue dragging across your cock as you thrust in and out of my warm, wet mouth?"

I drew his cock out of his pants with those last words, and it twitched in my hands, a drop of pre-cum beading at the tip. I went with my instincts, my need to taste him overriding any fear I had about not doing this right. I leaned forward and licked the drop off, the swipe of my tongue eliciting a groan from him.

I liked the sound so much, I did it again. Hearing his pleasure at that light touch was a heady thing.

"I'm not sure what I'm doing." I looked up to him through my lashes as I spoke, stroking him lightly with one hand while the other ran up the corded, taut muscles of his abs.

"All you have to remember is to be careful with your teeth. Other than that, you're free to do anything you want."

"That's what I like to hear." I grinned at him before looking back to his cock. I brought my second hand down to play, wrapping them both around him and marveling at how my fingers couldn't quite touch. My smaller hands gripping his cock, the head sticking out the top and leaking pre-cum was a sight I never wanted to forget.

After stroking him a few times like that, using the thumb nearest to his head to gather the leaking wetness and rub it around and learning what he liked best. I lifted his dick slightly and moved my hands so I could lick him from the bottom to top. After slowly making my way up, I went back down and then ventured further to run my tongue across his balls.

That move had Liam hissing and shoving his hands into my hair, pulling slightly and making my scalp tingle in a way that traveled down to my pussy. I could feel myself start to drip down the inside of my spread thighs, and I wondered if Liam could smell me.

I finally moved my tongue from his balls and went back up to the head, running my tongue around the top as I pumped his length with my hands. I wondered how long I could tease him like this before he snapped. After all, I owed him some payback for his stunt with my paintings.

With that wicked thought in mind, I continued to supply him with licks and light strokes, keeping him on the edge but never fully taking him into my mouth. Minutes passed, and his hands tightened in my hair whenever I touched a particularly sensitive spot just on the underside of the head.

Soon, my teasing was not even enough for me. I took the tip into my mouth, being careful not to use my teeth as I sucked on him lightly.

"Jesus fucking Christ, Celeste, you're killing me."

I popped him out of my mouth to look up at him. "Payback's a bitch, isn't it, Liam?"

A rough growl left him and goosebumps popped up on my skin.

"You've made your point, babe. Now please, take my dick in your mouth and suck me."

"Well, since you asked so nicely," I said in a sweet voice. And even though I'd never sucked cock before, I had figured out a long time ago that my gag reflex was nil. Something that Liam figured out very quickly when I took him all the way down my throat in one go.

I held him in the back of my throat, moaning as he cursed above me, loving the way his thighs began to shake when I swallowed hard around him.

God, I'd always wanted to try that. I'd just had no idea doing it would turn me on so much. Pulling away, his saliva covered cock slid out of my mouth into my hands, stroking him hard and fast as his hips began to thrust into my tight grip.

"I want you to fuck my face, Liam. Use those hands buried in my hair to hold me still and come hard into my mouth. I'm going to swallow you, and I'm going to touch my pussy as I do, so when I start to really moan as you use my mouth and throat, you know I'm coming with you."

"You're such a dirty fucking girl, Celeste. God, you're perfect."

With those words of praise that had me already rubbing my clit, he did just as I asked.

As he used my mouth for both our pleasure, his gritty words pushed me further towards climax. Tears gathered in my eyes and spilled down my cheeks, and it seemed to spur Liam on even more.

"Fuck, baby. Your mouth is so good. I'm not going to last long like this."

I'd already put him so on edge that with just a few strokes, he was gasping out his release, his salty-flavored come shooting into my mouth and down my throat. Just knowing he couldn't stop himself had me falling over the edge, one hand on my tit squeezing my nipple, the other with fingers flying over my clit to drag out my orgasm as much as possible.

Liam's hips stuttered, and I swallowed the last of him down as he slowly pulled out of my mouth. I licked my lips to make sure I hadn't missed anything, and Liam let out a little gruff moan at the sight.

"Greedy girl." His hands moved from my hair to cup the sides of my face. His thumbs passed over my cheeks to wipe away the leftover tears still there. "You doing all right?"

I nodded happily, basically purring as he caressed my skin. My eyes began to close, the adrenaline from everything that had happened tonight beginning to crash and catch up with me.

I heard Liam murmur something softly as he picked me up and gently placed me on his bed, but I was too tired to open my mouth and ask what he'd said before I fell asleep to him climbing into bed behind me and pulling me into his body.

———

I woke up the next morning with only a small headache left-over from my drinking the night before, and I was grateful I hadn't gone too overboard.

"You're finally awake," Liam rumbled in the sexiest morning voice I'd ever heard.

Turning in his arms to face him, I gave him a sleepy smile. "I am. What time is it?"

"Probably close to noon."

"Oops. I guess I was tired," I said with a laugh.

"You were. I let you sleep in a bit, but I had some food delivered about fifteen minutes ago. If you're hungry, feel free to go down and eat. I'm just going to shower really quick."

"Thanks, I will take you up on that offer." Liam leaned over me and kissed me, neither of us caring about morning breath apparently. He lifted off me with a light groan, evading my wandering hands.

"If you get your hands on me, we'll never leave this bed," Liam playfully scolded me as he walked towards the bathroom buck-naked. I gleefully took in the play of his muscles all the way down from his shoulders to his heels.

"What's so bad about that?" I quipped back.

"Get your ass downstairs and eat something, woman," he yelled before shutting himself in the bathroom. I laughed, but did as he asked. The nearest article of clothing was Liam's shirt from last night, so I shrugged and put it on, doing up a few buttons before making my way downstairs.

I loaded a plate with goodies and sat at the table, eating

mindlessly as I went through the events of last night. Liam had taken my paintings from the workroom and hung them up in the gallery for the showing, without my permission. I still felt a little bit betrayed that he went behind my back, ignoring my express wishes, but I had to admit that was mostly my pride and fear holding me back.

I'd been too afraid of rejection, to take a chance. Liam had seen that, and despite the risk had shown me I had what it took to be successful in something I loved. He showed me I was a beautiful, talented, and impressive woman all on my own.

So, although I'd been so close to throwing a major bitch fit in front of everyone there at the showing last night, I was so glad I'd controlled myself at the time. I mean, I got to meet freaking Serena Olivas! I shook my head in wonderment, recalling the way she'd talked about my art like it was something impressive. All in all, I was grateful to Liam for pushing me.

Having sorted through my feelings and realizing I'd eaten all my food, I didn't notice the woman standing there looking at me until I began to stand from the table. With a short shout, I jumped back and tumbled as my legs hit my chair. I managed to catch myself on the table without dropping my dishes, but that was the least of my worries.

In front of me stood Janet, Liam's mother. I quickly glanced over her, noticing not much had changed. She still wore expensive clothes and a tight, grim smile that I'm sure she thought was welcoming. She ran her eyes over me in return, eyebrows raising and saying everything her lips never would.

I suddenly remembered I was only wearing Liam's shirt. A hot blush spread over my whole body as I hurried to finish buttoning up his shirt so I wouldn't flash Janet like I'd almost done a second ago.

Thank God, I'd buttoned all the bottom ones.

"Well, I must say this was unexpected." Janet's haughty voice broke the awkward silence. "When I asked Liam to give you a job, I didn't mean for him to have you working *under* him."

Her harsh words were clear with a not-so-hidden meaning, and my flush grew hotter even as anger sparked in my chest.

"Whatever you're thinking happened is wrong, so you can calm down."

"Oh, you're saying you didn't spend the night in my son's bed? Your own *stepbrother's* bed?"

I opened my mouth to protest, but I couldn't technically say that was a lie. I had spent the night in his bed, it just wasn't the way she was thinking.

"You should be ashamed," Janet continued when I failed to speak up. "Your father would be so disappointed in you."

That did it. I stood up to my full height – which wasn't much, but it made me feel better – and spoke to her as evenly as possible.

"You have no idea what my father would think, because you were only married for six months before you left him."

"It was long enough to know he wouldn't want you to solve your problems this way, by whoring yourself out and sleeping around to make ends meet."

Her words struck me right in the chest, and my mouth gaped open. She seriously thought I was using my body to pay off my debts? That I was using Liam to do so? I hadn't gotten along with her a decade before, but now I *really* didn't like her.

"You don't know anything about me, or apparently about your son. I suggest you leave. *Now.*"

She scoffed. "Like Liam would want to spend his future with someone like you. You might be the forbidden fruit for him, but he'll set you aside once he's done admiring you like a piece of art at auction."

She turned and marched out the front door, leaving me with a split open heart in the middle of the kitchen. As much as I hated to think it, was she right? Liam hadn't spoken of any future with me, hadn't expressed any feelings besides desire. I was in love with him, and it was very possible it was all one-sided. I numbly moved my dishes to the sink, trying, and failing, to tell myself his mom was just a hateful woman who knew nothing about my and Liam's relationship.

My breathing picked up in anxiety, and I knew I needed to get out of there. I left the dishes in the sink and sprinted up the stairs. My house was done, ready for me to move back in, and suddenly I needed to be in my own space more than anything. I began to pack up my belongings, hoping to get out of there before Liam found me.

No such luck, of course. I was shoving the last of my clothes into my suitcase when he came up behind me, wrapping his arms around me and nuzzling into my neck.

I wanted to melt into him so badly I ached, but I stiffened my body in resolve.

"What're you doing, babe?"

I swallowed before answering, hoping my voice would stay steady. "I'm going home."

I could practically feel his warmth drawing away from me, his body going cold as he drew away from me. I resumed stuffing my suitcase, refusing to turn and look at him.

"I thought this was home."

"Is it? I'm grateful to you for giving me a place to stay. For showing me so much. But it's time I went back to my own life."

The finality in my own voice was hard to hear, but it was the emotionless tone of his that had my eyes watering.

"So, that's it then? You're just going to leave?"

I spun around to face him. "Why shouldn't I? Is there a reason I should stay?"

We searched each other's eyes for answers, but when I found none I sighed. "This is what's best for both of us. Thank you for... everything. I'll see you at work next week."

I couldn't look at him as I hoisted my bag off the bed and began to carry it down the hallway and stairs. I couldn't let him see my eyes overrun with tears as I left my heart in pieces in that room with him. Turns out I'd been the fool, falling in love with someone who didn't feel the same. It'd happened to my dad with Janet, and now it'd happened to me with her son.

Chapter 24

Liam

"Are you even listening to me, Liam?"

"Huh? Oh, sorry." I tried to focus on my mom, today's lunch appointment somehow harder than it'd ever been before.

Actually, I knew why. I'd been like this for the last two days, completely unable to concentrate on anything except trying to figure out what the hell had gone wrong with Celeste and me, what had made her leave so abruptly.

I'd come up with less than nothing. She'd been perfectly content before I stepped into the shower, and I'd come out to find her packing her shit and running out of there like Hell hounds were after her.

"If you're not going to pay attention to me maybe we should just reschedule."

Janet's words brought me out of my musings once again, and I flushed guiltily.

"Sorry, just have a lot on my mind." I grabbed my water and gulped some, hoping it would help clear my head.

"Hmph. What's that tart of a stepsister done now?"

I nearly choked on my drink. "What did you just say?"

"Oh please, no need to be coy. I walked in on her wearing nothing but your shirt, and it wasn't even decently buttoned. I think it's shameful that you've let her get under your skin. She's only getting close to you so she can manipulate you."

I stared at her, wondering if she was joking or not. The idea of Celeste manipulating me for her nefarious ways, as my mother was implying, was so ludicrous I began laughing.

"Surely, you don't find that harlot using you to be funny, Liam Alexander."

My laughter stopped cold, and I glared at my mother with eyes like slits. "First of all, if you ever call her a harlot, tart, or any other disparaging names, we are through. I don't care that you're my mother. I won't have you talking that way about a woman I love."

Janet's eyes had gone wide with surprise, and she blinked at me while processing my threat.

"You really do care about her."

"Of course. When have I ever let a woman move into my house, stepsister or not? Which, by the way, has no real bearing on our relationship because we barely even saw each other in the short time you and her dad were married. It sounds scandalous, but in reality it means nothing."

Expecting an immediate response, since that was her usual M.O., I was slightly surprised to see her expression turn nervous and noticed she seemed to be chewing on the corner of her lip. A weird foreboding filled me, and suddenly her words from before made me realize I was about to figure out the missing piece of information I'd been trying to find since Celeste left.

"Janet, when you said you walked in on her wearing nothing but my shirt, what did you mean?"

"Well, I stopped by a couple of days ago. I knocked, but

no one answered. I saw your car in the driveway, so I decided to let myself in just in case something bad had happened."

She trailed off, and I cleared my throat loudly to make her continue.

"When I walked in and saw Celeste sitting at your table, bare except for your shirt, I was sure she was using her... self... to convince you to help her out. Financially."

Shame colored her cheeks, as it well should. I was boiling with anger, realizing my mother had made Celeste second guess everything we'd shared in a few, short minutes with her clever barbs.

"Listen very closely. I love Celeste, and I'm pretty sure she loves me too. She's the most kind-hearted, selfless, humble woman I've ever known. She would *never* do what you're suggesting, and the fact you think I can't spot a gold digger of a woman from a mile away, after being raised by one, is embarrassing. So, I suggest you think of a way to apologize for all of this if you want to stay in my life, because Celeste is the center of that for me."

With that, I stood from my chair, threw some money on the table and stormed out to my car. I was fuming, and I needed to cool down. I took the next few hours to drive around and figure out what my next step would be. I still hadn't really come up with a solution when I went back to the office, surprised to see Travis' car still there at the late hour.

I called out his name as I walked in the building, and he came out of his office with bleary eyes.

"Fall asleep again?"

"Yep," he confirmed with a sheepish smile. He had a habit of doing that when he stayed later than everyone else. "What're you here for?"

"Forgot some stuff earlier," I grunted, but didn't move toward my office to get anything. Travis' eyes began to clear, and as he looked me over, he sighed.

"All right, come on in and get a drink. You look like you need it."

It wasn't until my second glass of whiskey that I was able to tell him what happened without wanting to go and strangle my mother. When I finished the story, I gave Travis a moment to think about his response before giving it. However, the first question he asked wasn't what I was expecting to hear.

"Do you love her?"

"Yes." No hesitation.

"Does she know?"

"Of course, after everything I've done for her. She should."

"That's all well and good, but have you actually told her?"

"Yes, I tol—" I paused suddenly, thinking about it. Fuck, he was right. I hadn't actually said the words to Celeste.

"There's your answer right there. Go find her and tell her you love her, you big idiot."

If desperation to find her hadn't been clawing at my chest, I would have laughed. As it was, I could hear Travis chuckling as I left my barely touched drink on the desk and bolted out of there.

"Celeste, if you're in there, please just let me in!" I was pounding on the front door of Celeste's house, begging her to let me in so I could fix things. I was trying to keep my voice low so as not to disturb her neighbors since it was late, but I'd rather make a fool of myself at that point than to leave without telling her how I felt.

There were lights on, but I hadn't heard or seen any movement in the house. It was possible she was avoiding me, but I was beginning to think she wasn't even here. Looking around to make sure no one was watching, I walked to the side of the house where she would usually keep her car in the port. I peeked through the window, and my suspicions were confirmed.

Wondering where she could have gone this late at night, I pulled out my phone and tried to call her. I leaned against my car as the phone rang in my ear, leg bouncing on the sidewalk while I tried to stay patient.

"Hi! You haven't quite reached Celeste, but if you leave your deets at the beep then I'll get back to you in a jiffy!" I hung up before the tone, hitting the redial button. I did that twice more before figuring she was ignoring me.

Dejectedly, I got back in my car and headed home, dialing her a few more times before giving up as I turned onto my street. Letting it go to voicemail, I decided to leave a message this time.

"Hey Celeste, I need to talk to you. Give me a call when you get this message. Or you can text me. Or, hell, I don't know. Attack me at work or something because I need to talk to you more than anything. Please."

I hung up, turning into my driveway. I stomped on my brakes when I saw a very familiar car sitting there already. The shock wore off in a second, and I was out of my car before it even finished turning off. I burst through my front door and followed the sounds of rummaging to my room.

"Celeste," I breathed out in utter relief as I saw her there, arms full of random clothes she'd left here in her hurry to go. I walked towards her, barely registering the shock on her face to see me there. In a second, I had her in my arms, clothes and all, breathing in her familiar scent.

"Liam, I can't breathe."

Realizing I was squeezing the life out of her, I loosened my arms and helped steady her on her feet.

"What was that all about?"

Elation filled me at seeing her back in my house, even though it looked like she'd merely come to grab the rest of her things and make her escape. I couldn't help the giant grin that split my face when I said, "You mean I can't hug the woman I love just because I'm overjoyed to see her?"

Celeste drew in a sharp breath, beautiful aquamarine eyes widening at my words. "You... what?"

"I love you, Celeste Thompson. I've been such a fucking idiot for not telling you sooner. I should've said it weeks and weeks ago when I realized I was falling for you. I'm so sorry my mother said such horrible things to you, but I need you to believe I have never thought about you like that."

Her eyes turned liquid, and she hugged the clothes in her arms tighter to her, like she was bracing for something. "You love me?"

"How could I not? You're the most incredible woman I've ever met. I've been obsessed with you since the moment you came back into my life, and before that even. I don't just love you; I need you. The last two days have been hell without you."

"Oh, Liam," she cried in a cracking voice as she dropped everything in her arms and launched herself at me. I caught her easily and covered her mouth with my own.

I grabbed a handful of her hair and carefully pulled her away. "Tell me you love me too," I demanded, not giving her room to back out now.

"Liam. Of course I love you. I've loved you since I was fifteen and didn't even know what it meant. I was devastated when I thought you didn't feel the same."

"Promise me next time you'll talk to me before you up and go. I couldn't stand it if you left me again."

"Promise."

My mouth was already descending as she spoke, and I swallowed the word. Our hands roamed with a frenzy, grabbing and clutching each other with a need so strong it belied words. I somehow found the bed and fell back on it, letting her fall on top of me before I rolled us over.

Finally pulling away to catch our breath, we stared at each other, all the emotions running high between us and electrifying the air.

"You have all of me, Liam," Celeste whispered. "I need you to take it." I couldn't pretend I didn't know what she meant, and I knew I wouldn't be able to deny her or myself any longer; this was the moment the two of us had been waiting for all along. Pressing my lips against hers in a hard kiss, I let her know I understood. I was going to make this moment so fucking special for her, for the woman I loved who loved me back.

Chapter 25

Celeste

I trembled under Liam's drugging kiss, shivered with every brush of his fingers against my skin. Something in the air between us changed as he pulled back from the kiss. It felt more caring, more tender. My desperation from earlier had cooled a bit, and I watched with a content smile as Liam slid off me to stand next to the bed.

After what felt like a lifetime of waiting, this was happening.

My breathing sped up again as I watched Liam slowly undress, pulling his shirt off over his head and exposing his muscled chest to my greedy eyes. I followed each curve and dip, tracing that delicious 'V' that peeked out of his low-slung pants. His hands moved to undo his belt buckle, unbuttoning and unzipping his jeans before pushing them down his legs to pool on the floor. He stood before me in nothing but a pair of snug boxer briefs, the black fabric doing nothing to conceal the size and shape of him.

Remembering how it felt to have him between my lips, my

mouth watered and I would bet anything that the look in my eyes turned downright hungry.

"Oh no you don't, dirty girl. I'm saving this cock for that little pussy of yours."

A little moan escaped me, and the heat went up in the room another couple of degrees.

Liam reached for me and curled his fingers around the waistband of the exercise shorts I was wearing, pulling them and my panties right off me.

"Mmm, look how wet you are for me already. How bad do you want this?" he asked me, stroking his cock through his underwear in a move so unexpectedly erotic my heart stuttered in my chest.

"I want it so bad," I whispered in a rough voice. "I'm dripping for you, Liam."

"Fuck, yeah, you are," he said as he swiped two fingers through my juices in a quick move.

I gasped at the feeling, and again at the sight of Liam licking my taste off his fingers. The almost romantic mood from before was quickly dissipating, the need between us too great to stay sweet.

I needed him rough and dirty, all-commanding, and non-apologetic. I wanted him to sink so deep inside me that I ached from it the next day; and I could tell he wanted me the same way.

Sitting up slightly, I yanked off my top, leaving me bare since I'd gone sans bra. In the next second, Liam was pushing me farther up the bed, only stopping when he settled his pelvis against mine between my spread legs. He latched onto one of my nipples with lips and teeth at the same time he gave a wild thrust of his hips into mine.

"Oh God, Liam!" I gripped the bed sheets next to me, instantly wrapping my legs around Liam's moving hips and moving my own against him with just as much fervor.

"I meant to go slower, treasure you," he growled against my breast. The vibrations sent me higher, and I moaned again as he switched sides.

"I don't care about that. I just need you inside me. Now, please, please, please," I chanted in his ear.

"Shit baby, you drive me crazy." He pulled away from my tits and I rejoiced, thinking he was finally going to give me what I wanted. I was surprised to see him move lower down my body, and before I could voice a protest his mouth landed on my bare pussy.

Stars were already bursting behind my eyes as he ate me out, his tongue swirling around my entrance and teasing me with what I wanted. He swiped his tongue up to my clit, rubbing it on the more sensitive side, making me cry out as two fingers replaced the teasing of my pussy hole.

"You're so tight down here, baby, are you sure you're ready for my cock?" Slowly he pressed those fingers in, stretching me out.

"Yes," I cried out loudly. I wasn't sure if I was answering his question or telling him to keep pushing his fingers inside me. The stretch was tight, but it wasn't painful. I'd used vibrators before so I wasn't unfamiliar with the feeling.

What was unfamiliar was knowing that soon, his cock would be inside me, stretching me farther than ever before. The thought of taking him inside me, pressing deeper and deeper and not stopping even if I whimpered with discomfort, had my cunt gushing around Liam's fingers.

"Damn baby, what were you thinking about that got you wet like that?"

"You," I panted. "Inside me. Hurting so good. Not stopping."

His fingers had started rubbing against my G-spot while I was talking so my answer came in short bursts.

"So goddamn hot, Celeste. The sooner you come for me like this, the sooner I'll put my cock inside you like you want."

"God, yes." Two seconds later I burst, crying out his name as I pulsed around his fingers, his tongue laving my skin as he licked me clean.

I was still throbbing when Liam got to his knees and slung my thighs over his. I reached above my head and grasped the wooden slats of his headboard, arching my back and pressing my center closer to him.

"You're so fucking beautiful, Celeste." Liam ran his rough hands over my thighs, widening me even more. He kept one hand high on the inside of my thigh, his thumb pressing against the seam between my thigh and pussy. I tingled, watching as he grasped his cock and ran it up and down my slit, bumping my sensitive clit and making me jump a little with each pass.

I needed him to stop teasing me. I needed him to press inside me and be the first to break me open. I needed it so bad, and I was willing to play dirty to get it.

"Come on, Liam, don't you want to know what it feels like to fuck your stepsister? It's so bad, but it's going to feel so good."

"Filthy as fuck, baby. Now take your stepbrother's cock like the good girl I know you are."

With that, he pressed forward. I gasped as he breached my entry, this pressure different than any before it. I was prepared for pain, but as he slid deeper and deeper into me, all I felt was bliss. He leaned forward, curling himself around me and pressing the last bit of his throbbing cock into me.

"Jesus." He leaned his forehead on my shoulder, kissing my skin while he let me adjust around him. I wiggled underneath him, and he tightened his hands to hold me still. "Give me a sec, babe."

I giggled when I realized he wasn't moving because he

needed to control himself. "The big, bad man can't last longer than the virgin?"

He bit down on my shoulder, and that one thing caused a chain reaction in the two of us. I gasped, and my whole body tightened as the ripples of pain-turned-pleasure went through me. When my pussy squeezed around Liam's cock inside me, his hips jerked forward and thrust even deeper into me.

That one thing was all it took; suddenly he was pistoning inside me, grunting and groaning along with my every moan and cry. The head of him dragged across my sensitive walls, and all I could see, hear, feel, was Liam.

"Come for me, Celeste. Come with my cock deep inside your tight little pussy. I'm the first and the *last* man to ever be inside this cunt. Tell me, baby, say you're mine."

He reached down and rubbed my clit and I was there, legs shaking and cunt beginning to pulse around him.

"I'm yours," I yelled with a strained voice.

"Good girl. Now, let me feel you. Come all over my big cock, stepsister. *Now.*"

I detonated, my hands flying to his back and nails digging into his skin. He tensed, and I felt my pussy fill with warmth as his cum covered my walls and started to drip out around us. His shallow thrusts dragged out both of our orgasms until we were completely sated. He rolled to his side still in me, pulling me tight to his chest as our breathing calmed.

I ran my fingers up and down his side, more content than I'd ever been in my life.

"You're moving back in, right?"

My hands paused on his skin at the words, and I began to shake with laughter. I buried my face in his neck as I laughed.

"Oh my god, that's the first thing you say after that?"

"Well... yeah. I mean, how else are we supposed to do this all the time?"

Curbing my laughter, I pretended to think about it. "Hmm. You do have a fair point."

"That, and I love you and being apart from you sucks ass."

"Kinky."

"Wow, virgin one moment and wanting butt play the next. You really are filthy," Liam teased and smacked my ass playfully.

"You started it!"

"I'm finishing it too. You're moving in."

I stared at him, eyebrows raised and silence growing.

"Okay, okay," Liam relented. "But seriously, do you want to keep your house? I know it's important to you because of your dad, and I don't want to make you just give it up. But I would love for you to live with me here. Even if you don't decide tonight, will you think about it?"

"Of course," I replied. "I'll let you know what I decide."

"Awesome. How sore are you?"

I took a mental inventory. "Not too bad. Why?"

"Round two, baby!" I laughed as he wrestled with me in the bed, both of us trying to get the upper hand.

Best. Night. Ever.

One week later

"All right, this is the last box," Liam called out as he maneuvered said box through his front door. Both of us were slightly sweaty and breathless, having moved most of my stuff over to his place. It hadn't taken me long to say yes to him; I'd already figured out holding onto the house was more sentimental than economically wise. I didn't really need the house, and I wanted to be with Liam anyhow. The best memories I had of my dad were in my mind and heart, not the house.

"Thank you," I responded as I met him in the front room and grabbed it from him. I was setting it down when he came up behind me and ground his already hard cock into my ass.

"Wow, already?" I teased him, but honestly, watching his muscles bulge moving all my stuff around had gotten me turned on like crazy. Under my jean shorts and light pink underwear, I was wet as hell.

"I'm always ready for you, babe. Now, what do you say we christen this place?"

A throat clearing behind us interrupted my response, and both of us spun around guiltily. Seeing Liam's mother standing there was the last thing either of us expected.

"Sorry to interrupt, but I came by to... apologize."

I glanced up at Liam, seeing the abject surprise on his face. I was guessing this didn't happen very often. I turned back to Janet, giving her my full attention.

"I expected the worst of both of you, and it wasn't fair. Celeste, your dad was my only real support and help in the years I knew him, even after I left him. Being married to him was the best six months of my life, and I regret leaving him every day. I was scared to be as happy as I was, and I left before it could be taken away from me."

She paused here and pulled a handful of papers out of her purse. "By way of apology, and a belated thanks to your father, I'd like to give these to you."

I moved forward automatically and took the papers from her. It took me a second to realize what I was looking at, but when I did, the tears were already falling.

"I know it's just money, but I'd like to think it's a way to start over. For all of us."

"This is too much..." I said the words, my hands shaking and eyes clouding over as I looked over the multiple invoices with a PAID IN FULL stamp across the top. The house mortgage. The hospital bills. My student loans. All paid.

"It's not. After a few divorces that ended favorably for me, I have plenty to spare. Can we... put the past behind us? Try and start on a better foot?"

I finally noticed the nerves that laced her voice and looked up at her through the tears of relief and gratefulness. She was standing tall and proud, but her hands were clasped in front of her tightly.

I shoved the papers into Liam's hands and made it to her in just a few strides, throwing my arms around her stiff body.

"Yes, I would love that."

My words seemed to release the tension in her body and she loosened enough to hug me back, although I could tell the action was not a familiar one. I stepped away so I wouldn't be making her more uncomfortable than she already was, and she gave me a trembling smile.

"And Liam," she started as she turned to him.

"It's okay, Mom. All is forgiven."

I saw the tremble go through her, and knew she was doing everything she could not to fall apart in front of us. She'd apologized gracefully, but she was still a proud woman.

"Would you like to come over for dinner after we've got everything put back together?"

My invitation brought a smile to her face, softening the harsh lines that had grown over the years.

"Yes, please. I'll, uh, leave you kiddos to it then," she said with a small blush regarding the conversation she'd accidentally interrupted. "And next time, try to remember to shut the front door first."

Liam and I burst into laughter as she left.

"That was embarrassing," Liam chuckled.

"That, Liam, was a new beginning." We were obviously talking about slightly different things, but he agreed.

"Now, where were we..."

Epilogue

Four Months Later

Liam

F uck, I had never been this nervous. With the help of
Celeste's friends, whom I'd become close with in my
own right, we'd planned a welcoming back party for
Luke. Really, it was a cover. After all, Luke had been back for
a couple of weeks and we had all celebrated together. This
was really a surprise engagement party for Celeste and me.

And I was nervous because I hadn't proposed yet.
Everyone was waiting in the small event hall at our office, and
Celeste and I were walking down the hallway together. She
was chatting away about something from earlier in the day,
but I was so full of nerves I didn't hear a word. We were about
four feet from the door when I blurted out her name.

"Celeste!" I yelled it way too loud, and she jumped a bit at
the interruption. I stopped both of us, glancing at the closed
doors separating us from everyone else.

"I'm right here, you don't have to yell," she said with a laugh. "What's up?"

"I love you. You love me, right?"

"Yes..." she drew out the word, confusion on her face.

"That settles it! We're getting married."

"Well, where's my ring then?"

That startled me. I'd expected her to fight me at least a little. Hands shaking, I pulled the box out of my back pocket, opening it for her to see. Her eyes widened, her mouth forming a small 'O'.

"It's even prettier than Madison said," she breathed out.

"Wait, what?"

"Oops... Well, you should know Madison isn't the best secret keeper. Especially when I'm the interrogator." A smug smile tilted her lips up. "When you started acting all cagey, I started asking questions."

"You little brat," I said on a laugh. I wrapped my arms around her as I kissed her and smacked her bottom. She tilted her head and opened her mouth, swiping her tongue against my lips and asking for entry. I gave it to her, but only for a moment. We had a not-so-surprise party to attend, and I didn't need to walk in, full-on boner raging.

Celeste

I watched Liam talk and laugh with Luke, Anthony, and Travis with my heart so full of love I thought it would burst from my chest. We'd had a few more people here, but the men, Madison, and I were all who were left. Madison and I were standing by the bar, sipping water as we watched the men chat it up.

"Sorry I spilled the beans and ruined the surprise."

I turned to Madison with a smile. "No, you're not."

"You're right. I'm not at all. Did I tell you about the ring, or did I not?"

We both glanced down to the square cut aquamarine jewel that matched my eyes perfectly, the four corners embellished by tiny little diamonds all set on a platinum band. I usually didn't go for flashy things like this... but I could get used to it.

"You underestimated it, if anything."

"Well, I'm very glad to see you so happy, Celeste." Madison's words rang true, and if there was a tinge of sadness in her eyes, I did her a kindness by not mentioning it.

"Thank you," I replied, then hugged her tight. "Don't worry, Mads, you'll get your happy ending too."

She hugged me tight, then stepped back. "All right, enough of this! Let's go over there and bug the men."

"Deal." We linked arms and started towards the men. Liam immediately focused on me, and giant grins split both of our faces. I was walking towards my forever, and I couldn't wait for it to start.

Blushing Books

Blushing Books is the oldest eBook publisher on the web. We've been running websites that publish steamy romance and erotica since 1999, and we have been selling eBooks since 2003. We have free and promotional offerings that change weekly, so please do visit us at http://www.blushingbooks.com/free.

Blushing Books Newsletter

Please join the Blushing Books newsletter
to receive updates & special promotional offers.
You can also join by using your mobile phone:
Just text BLUSHING to 22828.

Every month, one new sign up via text messaging will receive
a $25.00 Amazon gift card, so sign up today!

www.ingramcontent.com/pod-product-compliance
Lightning Source LLC
Chambersburg PA
CBHW020637180626
46816CB00003B/1004